Happy reading!

SKYWAKE: INVASION
GO WITH THE FLOW!

WALKER BOOKS

SKYWAKE
BATTLEFIELD

JAMIE RUSSELL

WALKER
BOOKS

For Louise, for everything

First published 2022 by Walker Books Ltd
87 Vauxhall Walk, London SE11 5HJ

2 4 6 8 10 9 7 5 3 1

Text © 2022 Jamie Russell
Cover illustration © 2022 James Fraser

This book has been typeset in Berkeley Oldstyle

Printed and bound by CPI Group (UK) Ltd, Croydon CR0 4YY

British Library Cataloguing in Publication Data:
a catalogue record for this book is available from the British Library

ISBN 978-1-4063-9752-9

www.walker.co.uk

THE STORY SO FAR...

Fifteen-year-old Casey Henderson has discovered that her favourite video game, *SkyWake*, isn't just a game. It's actually a secret alien training tool.

Invited to a London shopping centre to take part in an eSports tournament to find the best *SkyWake* players, Casey met her online *SkyWake* team in real life for the first time. During the tournament, the true nature of the game was revealed when alien invaders known as "Red Eyes" took over the building and abducted the players, including Casey's little brother, Pete.

Using the knowledge they'd built up from playing the game, Casey and her team fought back with the help of military officer Lieutenant Dreyfus. In battle, Casey discovered the power of "flow" – a state of mind where you're totally focussed and in the zone – that gave her the confidence to lead her team.

After a final showdown on the aliens' ship, Casey and her friends were stranded on a planet called Hosin. Here the Red Eyes are planning to use their new army of mind-controlled human gamers as soldiers in a war against the mysterious, telepathic "Squids".

Stuck on this distant alien planet, Casey and her friends must find a way to survive the war and get back home. There's just one question.

Which side should they be on?

0

INSTALLATION COMPLETE

If Casey had known *SkyWake* was going to take over her life, she would never have started playing it. The mysterious first-person shooter had arrived at the beginning of the year, without any fanfare, as a free-to-play download. Within a week, it had gone viral and become a phenomenon. Overnight, gamers abandoned the big triple-A titles, from *Call of Duty* to *Fortnite*. Everyone wanted to be a *"SkyWaker"*.

Casey had always loved first-person shooter games, especially the immersive feeling of seeing the world through someone else's eyes. It made you feel like you were there, inside the virtual world, living every moment.

That was why, when she first downloaded *SkyWake*, she felt a tingle of excitement as the installation bar inched towards 100%. When it was ready, a title screen appeared showing a sleek black alien helmet with two piercing red eyes that stared out of the monitor at her with smouldering intensity. It took her a moment to realize they were subtly animated to give them a menacing flicker.

She clicked **NEW GAME** and pulled on her headphones. An animated cut-scene set up the story as words scrolled across the screen

Far across the galaxy, two alien races, the Arcturians and the Bactu, are locked in a deadly war. The Arcturians are searching for an ancient Bactu artefact called the "psionic array". If they find it—

Blah, blah, blah. Casey tapped the start button impatiently, cutting off the intro sequence in midflow. The story could wait. She just wanted to play.

A new screen appeared, asking her to select a faction. The Arcturians looked human and had jet-black power armour. Their mortal enemies, the Bactu, were squid-like creatures with pale blue skin, enormous bulbous heads and slithering tentacles. She wasn't sure which side to choose.

A hand tapped her shoulder, making her jump. Pete, her younger brother, had padded into her bedroom. Casey pulled off her headphones, trying not to let her irritation show.

"Can I play?" he asked.

"I haven't even started yet," Casey replied, wishing he'd stop ignoring the WARNING: NO STUPID PEOPLE BEYOND THIS POINT sign that hung on her bedroom door. He didn't seem to realize that she'd put it there especially for him.

"You should be those dudes in the black armour," Pete told her, jabbing a finger at the monitor. "They look cool."

"I was going to play as one of these squid things."

"Nah," Pete replied, reaching over her shoulder to tap the button to select the Arcturians. "Everyone says these Red Eye dudes are the best."

The next screen was a loadout menu. While Casey chose her soldier's class and equipment, Pete picked up a bottle from her desk and gave it a shake.

"Bubblegum Blue?" he said, reading the label. "Are you dyeing your hair?"

Casey snatched the bottle back. Then she remembered what her mum always told her: *Take a breath. Breathe out. Smile. Restart.*

"Why don't you come back later?" she suggested.

Pete ignored the hint. "What class you gonna be?"

he asked, pulling on the back of her gaming chair like he was steering an aeroplane. He was four years younger than Casey, was small for his age and could be annoyingly persistent.

"Assault, of course. Can you really see me as a hacker or a medic?"

"You should go sniper."

"Someone's already a sniper."

"Go tank, then."

"This guy called **FISH _ HEAD _ 04** is playing tank." She pointed to the list of gamertags as the game found other players on the *SkyWake* servers. "Now please go away."

"I want to watch," Pete said. "I heard those squid things have telepathic powers. They look well creepy."

"Please," Casey repeated. "I'll give you a shout when it's your turn." She knew he'd spend the whole match jabbering advice, pointing at the screen over her shoulder and putting her off her game. Sometimes he drove her mad.

The game's matchmaking system finished finding players. A giant structure appeared on-screen, gracefully orbiting an alien planet. It twirled and spun against a backdrop of twinkling stars.

"That's the orbital command station," Pete told her,

breathless with excitement. "The Red Eyes control the battle from there."

"Like a space station?" Casey asked. She wasn't sure how he knew all of this. YouTube, probably. Their mum didn't like him playing shooting games, but he was obsessed with watching videos about them.

"Yeah, and these ships here drop you into the battle." He tapped the screen as a fleet of dropships emerged from the space station and headed towards the planet.

The cut-scene moved inside one of the dropships. Within its belly Casey saw dozens of Red Eye soldiers stepping into egg-shaped pods, which closed behind them. As the cut-scene ended, she found herself in first-person mode, sealed inside one of the pods, staring through her soldier's eyes. She looked around using her controls, then down at her soldier's black-gloved hands. The dropship launched and headed out of the space station.

"What do you think Dad would have thought of this?" Pete murmured, leaning over her shoulder. Casey felt a sharp pang of sadness. She'd never know what he'd think of this one. Their dad, a soldier with the Royal Engineers, had loved video games. He'd been killed while serving in Afghanistan, defusing a car bomb planted outside a school.

A robotic voice interrupted them. *"Preparing drop pod launch. On my mark: five, four, three, two, one … DROP!"* There was a judder as dozens of pods blasted out of the ship, barrelling towards the alien planet below.

"This is it!" Pete shouted.

"Let me focus," Casey said, pulling her headset back on. Her eyes narrowed as she stared at the screen. She was about to play her first game of *SkyWake*.

Little did she realize that one day she'd be living it for real…

1

RED EYES DON'T SURF

Of all *SkyWake*'s maps, Casey liked the beach assault best. It was deceptively simple. You hot-dropped from orbit onto the Squids' home world, Hosin. Then you and your Red Eye squad advanced towards the enemy's base in the cliffs at the top of the beach. The map was epic in scale, a sprawling, full-frontal assault like an alien version of the D-Day landings. There was only one rule: keep moving or die.

Now, standing on the strange purple sand of the beach in real life, Casey was paralysed with fear. The moment her drop pod opened, she'd been hit by a wall of sound. Plasma fire and artillery exploded left and right. Red Eye fighter jets screamed overhead, cannons blasting as they fired at the Squids' positions. It was like watching an intense war movie in the cinema, the Dolby speakers cranked up to full volume.

More pods crashed onto the beach around her. The teen gamers that the Red Eyes had snatched from Earth stepped out, wearing exo-suits and combat helmets and carrying weapons that Casey and her team were used to seeing on their *SkyWake* screens. Unlike Casey, they didn't stop to stare in amazement at their surroundings. Instead, they advanced in squads, their faces blank as if they were under some kind of mind control.

A piercing screech roared above her and then there was a huge explosion as a Squid artillery shell landed beside her, blasting a plume of green plasma and purple sand into the air. Casey ducked as debris rained down around her, falling back to the earth.

No, she realized with a gasp, *not Earth.*

Hosin.

She was on the Squids' home world, light years from Earth, in the middle of a war between two alien species. She tilted back her combat helmet and wiped sweat from her forehead, feeling the heat of the two suns in the sky above her – one vast and pink, the other smaller and more of an orangey red. Behind her the waves rolled onto the beach, their rhythmic sound drowned out by the chaos of the battle.

Questions overwhelmed her.

How can this be real? Where are my friends?

And, most important of all…

How can I get home?

Her gloved hands tightened around her plasma rifle. There was something reassuringly familiar about it. She'd stood here holding a weapon like this a million times before when playing *SkyWake*. The game had trained her for this moment, giving her everything she needed to survive on this beach. She remembered the battles she'd fought here against the Squids. She knew that right now they would be slithering around in their tunnels under the sand, waiting to attack. The thought of them made her pause.

What did the Bactu want? Were they *her* enemies? She didn't know.

"Casey!" Her little brother's voice jolted her back to her senses. His drop pod had landed a few metres away from hers and he'd stepped out into the chaos, his face ashen with fear. "What should we do?"

They both ducked as two Phantom attack ships whooshed through the sky with a deafening sonic boom, their smooth metal underbellies almost close enough to touch. Casey glimpsed a Red Eye pilot in the cockpit of each as they passed overhead. A moment later, the ships raked the Squids' bunkers with their plasma cannons.

"We've got to move," Casey said, remembering the rule of the beach. She grabbed Pete's hand and looked around. The rest of her online teammates, the Ghost Reapers, were stepping out of their drop pods and staring at the battlefield in open-mouthed amazement. She only knew them by their gamertags, but that didn't matter – they had become her friends: FISH _ HEAD _ 04, XxxELITESNIP3RxxX, SPOCK5 _ BR@IN and CH33ZEMUNK3Y.

"Fish! she yelled, calling to the stocky, sandy-haired Glaswegian boy who played as the team's tank. "Get your shield up!"

"This is mental," Fish muttered, taking in the carnage. "How can this place be real? I thought it was just a map in the game."

"Focus!" Casey shouted, grabbing his arm. "We need your shield to stay alive."

The urgency in her voice did the trick. There was a crackle as Fish activated his energy barrier. It sprang out in front of him in a huge, protective rectangle of shimmering light.

"Everyone on me," Casey ordered, dragging Pete behind the cover of the shield. The rest of the boys fell in behind her.

Elite, the wannabe emcee from South London,

brought his sniper rifle up and peered down its scope as he scanned the vast expanse of beach that lay ahead. *"Yo, yo, my name's Elite,"* he rapped under his breath, trying to steel his courage. *"I got sick rhymes, don't need to cheat."*

Brain, a Black teenager from Leeds and the eldest in the group, held his medic's tool in one hand and an energy sword in the other. He was ready to patch up anyone who needed help. "Why are you rapping?" he snapped.

"Busting rhymes helps me focus."

"Well, it doesn't help me. Turn your comms off!"

The last to get into formation was Cheeze. He was still wearing the Red Eye power armour he'd hacked into after his wheelchair was destroyed in the shopping centre. It allowed him to walk, but the alien suit wasn't designed for humans. He staggered unsteadily across the sand, clearly in a lot of pain.

Casey noticed how easily the boys fell into playing their game roles. She guessed their training was kicking in too. All those hours spent in their bedrooms playing *SkyWake* had taught them everything they needed. She wondered where Lieutenant Dreyfus was. The soldier had been with them when they dropped from the Arcturian ship, but he was nowhere to be seen now. Had something happened to his pod in the descent?

The heads-up display on her helmet visor flickered into life, interrupting her thoughts. A mini-map appeared in her field of vision. It was exactly like the display on her monitor when she played *SkyWake*. A bright red waypoint directed them to the enemy objective further up the beach. She guessed this was what all the human gamers were seeing. Unlike the others, though, the Ghost Reapers had evaded the mind-controlling device the Red Eyes had tried to implant in their brains. They were free to make their own choices.

But what choices would keep them alive?

Casey realized the boys were all looking at her, expecting her to take charge. She'd always been their squad leader when they played together online.

She wet her lips, trying not to sound as scared as she felt. "Let's move," she ordered over her helmet's comms. "Fish, advance towards the next bunker. We'll try and take shelter in there. Brain, cover the right flank. Elite, cover our left. Watch out for sentry turrets behind that sand dune. Cheeze, cover our six. Let's go."

"What about me?" Pete asked, clinging onto her as another shell exploded near by.

Casey drew her plasma pistol from the leg holster on her exo-suit and passed it to him. "Just stay close," she said. "We'll get out of this, I promise."

Pete took the gun and stared at it. She momentarily considered giving him her exo-suit, too. But she knew she needed it herself. Without it to protect and augment her body, there was no way she could do her job as squad leader.

She swallowed hard.

This wasn't *SkyWake*. This was real. With no respawns. Was she really responsible for keeping her teammates alive? In the shopping centre she'd fallen into being the leader thanks to her skill with the plasma rifle and that strange sensation of "flow" she'd discovered while fighting the Red Eyes. Out here, though, the stakes were much higher. She'd been lucky so far, but sooner or later she'd make a mistake or a bad decision … and then what?

Casey brought her squad to a halt beside a Red Eye troop carrier. *SkyWake* players dubbed them "Rhinos" because of their heavily armoured sides. This one, though, was now little more than a smoking wreck after being hit by an artillery shell. Motionless Red Eyes lay on the sand beside it, their black suits reflecting the flicker of the green, plasma-tinged flames.

Further up the beach, Casey could see hundreds of teen gamers marching resolutely forward, ignoring the artillery shells exploding all around them.

Elite stared down his sniper scope, picking out their faces. "Red Eyes brought a whole army from Earth. It's like the United Nations out here."

It was true. The teenagers had been snatched from cities all around the globe: London, New York, Madrid, Seoul, Dubai and Johannesburg. They stayed in their squads, moving with uncanny precision as they took out the automated sentry turrets that the Squids had buried in the sand to deter invaders. Casey watched as one squad stormed a Squid bunker, shouting instructions to one another in clipped Spanish. They moved with single-minded purpose, unfazed by this strange alien planet.

"What's wrong with them?" Casey murmured as the Spanish gamers came back out of the bunker, their weapons smoking, and headed up the beach. They didn't even glance at Casey and the Ghost Reapers.

"They're mind-controlled," Pete said. "The Red Eyes put devices inside their helmets before we left Earth. I saw it."

Casey looked at her little brother. She realized she still hadn't had a chance to catch up with him properly.

What had happened to him back in the shopping centre? What had he been through without her?

"We've got to free them," Brain said, pushing his glasses up his nose. The lenses were covered in sand from the beach. "With their help, maybe we could overpower the Red Eyes."

Casey could see the logic. Brain deserved his gamertag.

"Why us?" moaned Fish. "We should just find somewhere to hide. Wait to be rescued." He pulled out his phone and tapped at the screen.

"Who are you gonna call?" Casey asked testily. "The police? The military? We're on an alien planet on the other side of the galaxy. Even if you had reception, they couldn't do anything."

"I just wanted to speak to my dad," Fish mumbled, his voice cracking slightly.

Casey felt bad for snapping at him. She had a sudden image of hundreds of parents back on Earth realizing that their children had been snatched and there was nothing they could do about it. She thought of her own mum. It was almost too much to bear. She pushed the thought out of her mind; she had to focus.

"We're going to get home," she told Fish, bumping her fist against his arm reassuringly. "I promise."

Her teammate nodded, rubbing his eyes.

"Any idea where they're getting their orders from?" Casey asked the others. Brain shrugged and deferred to Cheeze, the group's tech expert. The boy in the Red Eye power suit mopped his brow. He was being roasted alive in there.

"It could be a command-and-control system," he said thoughtfully. "I'll need to get a better look at that thing on their heads before I can work it out."

"Do you think that if we found the source of the signal, we could turn it off?" Casey asked.

The two boys looked at one another. They clearly thought it was possible.

"Hey," Elite said. He still had his sniper scope pressed against his eye and was scanning the beach. "We know this dude. I'll light him up."

He hit a couple of buttons on his scope and the squad's heads-up displays glowed as a silhouette appeared around the boy he was watching. The boy's squad was in a crater caused by a shell on the far side of the wrecked Rhino, pinned down by two automated sentry turrets that had emerged from the sand on the rim of the crater. The squad's tank player was waiting for his shield – depleted by the turrets' fire – to recharge before they advanced.

"It's Xander!" Casey exclaimed, recognizing the famous YouTuber's distinctive fringe. He was surrounded by his Strike Force teammates. The Ghost Reapers had lost to them in the *SkyWake* tournament back on Earth, just before everything kicked off with the Red Eyes.

"Are you sure?" asked Pete. He wasn't wearing a helmet and didn't have the benefit of the heads-up display. He tugged at his sister's arm. "If it's him, we've got to help them. He saved my life."

Casey looked at her brother in surprise. She guessed Xander must have taken Pete under his wing in the chaos in the shopping centre back on Earth. Perhaps the pro-gamer wasn't as much of an egomaniac as she'd first thought.

"Change of plan, everyone. Let's free Xander's squad first. Maybe we can find out from them what's going on. Elite, keep those sentry turrets busy. Fish, on me."

With that, Casey burst out from behind the wrecked Rhino, sprinting towards the crater. Fish stumbled behind her. As they approached the edge, the sentry turrets on the rim of the crater turned towards them. Before they could fire, a plasma shot rang out.

"Booyah," Elite cackled over the comms as the first turret exploded. "This sniper rifle is even sicker in real life than in the game!" There was a click as he reloaded. Then he took out the remaining turret. "Threat neutralized!"

Casey sprinted faster now the danger was gone. Down in the crater, Xander was signalling his squad to move out. He didn't seem to care how the turrets had been destroyed. He just wanted his squad to advance. They reminded Casey of video game AI characters, programmed to keep moving forward along a preset pathway.

The Strike Force players obediently scrambled up the crater's sloping sides and out onto the sand. The tank player's shield had recharged and he held it in front of them as they pushed on. Xander was bringing up the rear, his heavy combat boots struggling to find a foothold in the tumbling purple sand.

"Do you know how to rugby-tackle?" Casey shouted over her shoulder at Fish as they raced towards the YouTuber.

"Yeah, but who plays rugby on an alien beach?"

"We do!" Casey said, and launched herself at Strike Force's leader before he could escape.

2

THE LIGHTS ARE ON
BUT NOBODY'S HOME

Casey and Xander fell onto the sand at the bottom of the crater in a tangle of arms and legs. The YouTuber fought like someone possessed, driven by whatever all-consuming orders the Red Eyes were beaming into his brain.

"Get off me!" he yelled, thrashing wildly.

At seventeen, Xander was bigger and stronger than Casey with a gym-toned physique. She knew she couldn't hold him for long. Just as she was losing her grip on the contours of his exo-suit, Fish dived on top of them both. Xander grunted, flattened by the impact.

"I've got him, Casey! Get clear."

Panting, Casey commando-crawled from under the boys. She turned, breathless and bruised, to see Fish straddling Xander in the centre of the bomb-blasted crater. He'd pinned the YouTuber to the ground.

"Scrum half, first squad," he grinned. Beneath him, Xander stopped fighting and fell still, like a robot entering hibernation mode. Casey knew he would spring back into life the second Fish relaxed his hold.

A barrage of artillery fire whistled over their heads as the rest of the Reapers and Pete dropped into the crater. The plasma shells exploded on the beach above them in a percussive cacophony. The crater shook from the impact, but its depth kept the gamers safe. Xander's Strike Force comrades continued up the beach, marching through the clouds of green plasma gas without even flinching. They didn't seem to care that Xander wasn't with them. Getting to the objective at the top of the beach was their only concern. But what were they going to do when they got there?

"Squids ain't happy we destroyed their turrets," Elite shouted, holding his combat helmet in place as a shower of debris rained down on them. The familiar smell of bitter almonds filled the air as the plasma burned hot.

Casey grabbed Xander by the harness on his exo-suit and tried to shake some sense into him. Pete peered over her shoulder.

"Xander!" she shouted. "Can you hear me?"

"Take the objective," the YouTuber muttered. "Take the objective." His eyes were distant and glassy.

"Well, that's seriously weird," said Cheeze.

"Check under his helmet," Pete instructed.

Casey unclipped the chinstrap on the YouTuber's combat helmet and pulled it off. A strange device, like a high-tech hairnet, was clamped tightly to Xander's skull. It was covered in tiny red LED lights that flickered and flashed.

Brain leaned in to study the device. "It looks like it's monitoring the neural activity in his cognitive centres."

"What's that mean in English, bruv?" Elite panted.

"You were right," Casey said, glancing at Pete. "They're mind-controlling the gamers and getting them to attack the Squids. The gamers are like their puppets."

"Told you so!" Pete said. "The Red Eyes put them on all the gamers back on the dropship."

The hairnet was pinned tightly in position, by sharp prongs piercing Xander's scalp. His hair was crusty with dried blood.

Cheeze crouched down to examine the device. "I don't think we can get it off without hurting him."

"Can you hack it?" Casey asked.

"Maybe…"

"Let's take him with us then, and we can—"

Casey stopped abruptly, the words catching in her throat. Her head swam and, for a moment, she thought she might faint. The crater was spinning around her. She could see Cheeze looking at her uneasily. She reached out a hand to the sand to help her keep her balance.

It must be the adrenaline, she thought. She'd been running and fighting for hours, and her body had probably had enough. She tried to catch her breath, her heart pounding in her chest.

Then she heard the voice.

Casey…

It sounded strange and muted, as if coming from far away. No, she thought, that wasn't right. It didn't *sound* like anything. It seemed to jump directly into her mind, the words forming without making any noise whatsoever.

It felt wrong.

It felt … other.

Don't be scared.

Casey shook her head. For a moment she thought her comms device was malfunctioning and she was hearing random words from someone else's radio conversation. But the voice was insistent. It tunnelled into her consciousness, burrowing deep into her mind like a mole under a lawn.

We won't hurt you.

"Who are you?" Casey whispered.

We need your help.

A hand gripped her arm, distracting her. Pete was standing close, looking into her face, his eyes wide with concern. Her brother was saying something, but his voice seemed muffled as if she was underwater. She felt the strange presence in her mind recede.

"Casey?" Pete's voice was crystal clear now. "What's wrong?"

"Are you OK?" Cheeze asked gently. "You kind of zoned out. What happened?"

The boys exchanged worried glances.

"I don't know," Casey murmured. "I felt dizzy and…" She wasn't sure how to describe it. "I'm fine," she said, getting back on her feet as steadily as she could. "I could just do with some food."

"Tell me about it," Fish said, glancing at his belly.

"We should move," Casey said firmly, remembering the rule of the beach: keep moving or die. "We've been here too long." Her desire to get moving was more than that, though. The strange voice had unsettled her. She wanted to get away from it. If it was possible to get away from something that had appeared in her head out of nowhere.

At that moment, Xander jerked back into life. He shoved Fish off him and darted towards the side of the crater.

"He's making a break for it!"

Elite swung low as Xander passed him, going for his legs. Brain did the same and the pair ended up banging heads as they grabbed the fleeing boy. Brain's glasses flew off into the sand as Xander thrashed, trying to get free. Casey and Pete grabbed his arms.

"Don't stand on my specs!" Brain cried, patting the sand with his free hand as he tried to find his glasses. "I can't see anything without them."

A thundering noise shook the crater.

"Incoming!" Fish yelled, ducking in anticipation of another artillery strike. But this time the thunder didn't end in an explosive burst. It simply grew louder and louder, a deep bass that throbbed right through them as if they were standing next to a giant speaker playing dubstep. They looked up as an enormous black shape arrived, blocking out the two suns and bathing the crater in shadow. It was a Rhino.

The Red Eye troop transport was the size of a tank

with thick armoured sides, a heavy gun turret on its roof. As it rolled to a stop, Arcturian grunts leaped out of the vehicle and raised their plasma rifles. They stared down at the Reapers in the crater below them. One said something into his helmet communicator, talking in the Arcturians' spiky alien language.

The Reapers, caught off guard, stared in fear as a Red Eye approached them. He slid down the sloping side of the crater with ease, triggering a cascade of sand. Then he removed his helmet to reveal a familiar reptilian head. It wasn't a "he", it was a "she".

"Scratch!"

3

SHE LAUGHS,
BUT IT ISN'T FUNNY

The relentless Red Eye soldier the Ghost Reapers had fought in the shopping centre was unarmed. She didn't need a weapon when the rest of her squad stood on the lip of the crater with their plasma rifles at the ready.

Her mouth opened in a series of interlocking sections, revealing rows of white, lizard teeth. *"Ner hectan kindren corren ol,"* Scratch hissed in Arcturian and, as she spoke, a device clipped to her armoured breastplate translated her words.

"Only naughty children run away," it said, in stilted English. It sounded like an AI assistant running low on battery. Amused by her own joke, Scratch let out a strange sputter of croaks and rasps.

"She laughs," the translator said in a toneless voice, as if it was giving an audio description of a movie. But to the Reapers, staring into the barrels of the Red Eyes' guns, being able to understand the aliens' strange language wasn't funny. It was chilling. Casey guessed that the Arcturians must have scavenged the military's translation software from the shopping centre.

"I reckon I can take two of them," Elite muttered, one eye clamped to his sniper scope.

"That'll still leave another three," Brain snapped.

"I *can* count, bruv."

Scratch looked at the Reapers with hatred. Her lips curled with displeasure as she noticed Xander among their ranks.

"Release that soldier!" she instructed. "He has orders to wipe out our Bactu enemies."

"We can't do that," Cheeze said, stepping forward. He had his plasma rifle in his hands and was pointing it at Scratch's chest. She stared at him mockingly. Then, in a motion so swift it was a blur, she drew her energy sword from her belt. There was a whoosh as the blade of light formed. The sword slashed sideways, searing through the barrel of Cheeze's gun like a hot knife through butter. He stumbled backwards in surprise and fell onto the sand. Scratch towered over him, her obsidian eyes reflecting the fear that was spreading across his face.

"Didn't your mother teach you it's wrong to steal?" she sneered, staring at the power suit Cheeze was wearing. *Her* power suit. The one with the scratched breastplate. She spun the sword around in her hand with a flourish and pointed the tip at his throat.

"Don't hurt him!" Casey yelled. Scratch's face soured. For a moment, Casey thought the alien was going to launch herself at her in fury. Instead, she reached out a talon and took a lock of Casey's long hair. She ran her claw through it, admiring the bubblegum-blue streaks. The Arcturians, Casey noted, didn't have any hair at all.

"Cay See…" Scratch hissed, making Casey's name sound like two separate words. Then she continued in Arcturian, the device translating the rest of her words in its flat monotone. "I've been looking for you and your friends. I won't let you interfere on Hosin like you did on Earth. You cost me my promotion to overseer with your silly games. It's time for you children to be punished. All of you." She signalled to her troops. "Kill them."

Fish gave a startled whimper. "You can't kill us!" he said in disbelief. "We have rights!"

The Red Eyes' plasma rifles hummed. Casey felt her breath catch in her throat.

And that was when the Bactu attacked.

The crater shook as a Squid burst out, emerging from the ground as if it had been waiting for the right moment. Streams of purple sand cascaded over the creature's enormous bulbous head as it pulled itself up by its tentacles. Everyone was thrown off balance, as if caught in an earthquake.

The alien was the size of a minibus with an enormous orb-like eye on either side of its head. Its bluish skin was translucent, like the body of a glass frog, and you could see the outline of its internal organs beneath. It opened its beak, revealing rows of cracked and ragged teeth, and let out a high-pitched shriek.

Its tentacles flew out like flails. One sideswiped Scratch, knocking her off her feet. Others thrashed out at the Red Eye soldiers ranged around the lip of the crater.

"Run!" Casey yelled, hauling Pete off the sand and dragging him with her. A Red Eye who'd managed to get back on his feet started firing in their direction. The Bactu wrapped a tentacle around the soldier's ankle and carelessly flung him into the air. He landed in the crater beside Fish with a painful crunch. He didn't move again.

The rest of the Reapers were already crawling up the far side of the crater, slipping and sliding on the sand in their hurry. Cheeze and Brain pulled Xander between them, ignoring his attempts to get free. Whatever signal was being beamed into his brain was still calling him with its siren song.

A Red Eye tried to grab them as they fled, but Pete blasted him with his plasma pistol.

"Shot!" Elite shouted, impressed.

Casey didn't dare look back. She couldn't help but feel that the Bactu's arrival hadn't been a coincidence. Behind them, the Squid, scorched by plasma fire from the Red Eyes' guns, let out a deafening roar. There was a crunch as another soldier was thrown across the sand by its vicious tentacles.

"Where do we go?" Pete shouted as they reached the rim of the crater. He looked around the battlefield, the plasma pistol in his hand glowing hot. The battle was still raging as the squads of mind-controlled gamers continued to advance up the beach fighting the Squids' automated defences and dodging their artillery fire. Phantom attack craft whooshed overhead, raining bombs on the cliffs. The action in the crater was just a tiny moment in an epic battle, barely even worthy of a footnote amid the chaos that was unfolding.

Casey stared around the beach. "I don't know…"

Elite stumbled out behind her, followed by the

others. He nudged Casey with his elbow. In front of them, silhouetted against the sky, stood the Rhino that had transported Scratch and her squad. It had been left unguarded. Light from the pink and red suns glinted off its armoured body.

"Sweet wheels," he whistled. "Let's jack it."

4

GRAND THEFT ARCTURIAN AUTO

The five Ghost Reapers piled into the dark metal belly of the Rhino, bringing Pete and Xander with them. The vehicle was designed to take twenty soldiers across the battlefield and the interior was lined with simple flip-up seats, with a ladder in the centre that led to the gun turret on the roof. Up front was the driver's cab, with reinforced windows and a chunky steering wheel.

Casey and Pete guided Xander to a seat in the back. The YouTuber didn't resist. He seemed to have completely shut down, although the lights on the strange mechanical net stretched over his head still blinked and flashed. Cheeze fell into a seat beside Casey, his power armour juddering awkwardly as he sat down. He looked relieved to be off his feet.

Meanwhile, Elite, Brain and Fish crowded into the

Rhino's cab, barely able to contain their excitement as they pored over its high-tech dashboard.

"Who's driving?" Fish asked.

Elite pushed in front of him and slid his scrawny body behind the steering wheel. "Leave this to me."

"You can barely reach the pedals," Brain snorted.

Elite pulled the driver's seat forward as far as it would go. Which wasn't quite far enough. "My brother used to street-race round the back of our local retail park," he said. "I know how to motor."

"How old are you?" Brain demanded. "Thirteen?"

"Fourteen."

"Then you haven't even had a proper driving lesson yet!"

"How many have you had?"

Brain hesitated. "Two. But it's two more than you!"

Elite grinned, sensing victory. "What kind of car do they let you drive?"

"Erm … a Mini," Brain admitted. Fish stifled a laugh.

"What was that, bruv?" Elite asked, all innocent. "Didn't hear you."

"A Mini," Brain repeated. "But my instructor said I was a natural."

Elite waved him away. "Get out of here. No way driving a Mini will have prepped you for driving this beast." He stroked the steering wheel reverently.

"Can you stop arguing and get moving!" Casey shouted from the back. "That Squid won't keep those Red Eyes busy for ever."

Elite hit the dashboard and the Rhino lurched forward with a roar of power. Xander was thrown out of his seat and hit his head against the armoured wall. Pete ran to help him up and, as he did, he saw the hairnet on the YouTuber's scalp had been crushed by the impact. The LEDs flashed one last time and then died.

"Xander!" Pete yelled, shaking the YouTuber by the straps of his exo-suit armour. "Can you hear me?" He didn't respond, his face blank and impassive. Pete hauled him back into his seat. This time he made sure he strapped him in.

As the Rhino gathered speed, alarms screeched from the cab's dashboard. Casey could see Fish and Brain jabbing at the buttons, while Elite, who could barely see over the steering wheel, swerved across the battlefield. For a heavy vehicle, the Rhino was impressively fast and terrifyingly hard to control.

"What's that noise?" Elite shouted, too scared to take his eyes off the beach.

"Maybe there's a door open somewhere," Fish suggested. "That always happens in my dad's estate."

"Whatever it is, please turn it off," Elite begged. "I can't drive like this."

"Slow down!" Casey shrieked from the back. "You'll get us all killed."

The Rhino was now racing along the war-torn beach, the cliffs on one side and the sea on the other. Elite swerved past squads of mind-controlled gamers as they marched relentlessly across the sand. The teenagers moved methodically, taking out rows of sentry turrets and storming the Squids' defensive bunkers, which faced the shoreline. Automated plasma cannons inside each bunker unleashed stinging bursts of fire towards them. Casey wondered where all the Squids were. Other than the one in the crater, they hadn't seen any Bactu since they'd arrived. The mysterious aliens seemed to be hanging back, unwilling to engage the gamer invaders face to face.

The Rhino's alarms screeched on. Casey wasn't sure if it was her imagination, but could they be getting louder? Up in the cab, Brain stared at the dashboard and tried to decipher the alien symbols on the buttons.

"Why aren't you doing anything?" Fish shouted impatiently.

"I'm thinking it through logically," Brain replied. "If we list all the controls, we can work it out via a process of elimination. These buttons are for the weapons, these are for the drive system, these—"

"Sod that," Fish said and hammered the dashboard, hitting buttons at random.

"Wait!"

The alarms stopped.

"See?" Fish said, pleased with himself. His smugness didn't last more than a few seconds, though, as another alarm started to scream, angrier and louder than the last.

"Do something!" Elite yelled, swerving around a crater and narrowly avoiding tipping the Rhino into it.

"It must be one of these," Fish said, pressing the remaining buttons one after the other. The Rhino lurched and stuttered. The alarm continued to wail, like a banshee that had stubbed its toe.

"You're messing with the drive system!" Elite shrieked. Everyone was thrown sideways in their seats as he fought to keep control of the Rhino. Plasma fire from a nearby bunker raked the vehicle as it swept past. Brain continued to scrutinize the dashboard, then spotted something he hadn't noticed before.

"Er, guys," he said. "I think I know what the alarm is."

"Turn it off, then!"

"I can't. It's the enemy lock-on warning." He tapped the radar screen, where two red dots were flashing. "We've got company."

Elite glanced in the wing mirror. Two Phantom attack ships were barrelling through the alien sky towards them, plasma cannons spitting out hot death.

"Everyone, hold on!"

The Rhino zigzagged as the Phantoms strafed them. The plasma burned into the sand behind the vehicle, narrowly missing its chunky rear wheels.

"Casey! Get on the roof turret!" Elite shouted over his shoulder. Through the front windscreen they could all see the two Phantoms looping in the sky ahead, ready to make another attack run.

Casey unstrapped herself from her seat in the back and headed towards the ladder that led up to the gun.

"Be careful," Cheeze told her.

"Don't worry about me," she said, hiding her fear as best she could. "Just make sure Elite doesn't drive us into a ditch."

As she reached the ladder, Xander's eyes opened.

"Xander!" Pete cried. "You're back!"

The YouTuber smiled weakly and crossed his forefingers together to form his trademark "X" sign.

"Hey, buddy. Miss me?" He looked exhausted and pale, but much more like his old self. Pete copied the "X" gesture. Casey suspected her brother still hero-worshipped the arrogant YouTuber. She didn't know how she felt about it.

The enemy lock-on alarm screeched even louder as the Phantoms came in for another attack. Conversation would have to wait. Casey scurried up the ladder into the turret.

5

HOW AM I SUPPOSED TO CONCENTRATE WITH ALL THIS NOISE, PEOPLE?

Casey felt the humid beach air fill her lungs as she climbed the ladder onto the Rhino's roof. The turret was an armoured metal cylinder fitted with an enormous rail gun that *SkyWake* players called a BFG, or Big *expletive deleted* Gun.

As soon as she pulled the harness over her shoulders, her helmet visor patched into the gun's targeting system. She was assaulted by a barrage of flashing warnings as the computerized targeting system pinpointed the incoming Phantoms. She looked out over the alien battlefield, the beach peppered with destroyed Squid bunkers and the remnants of the Red Eyes' drop pods. She felt exposed up here.

"I can't shake them!" Elite yelled over the comms as more Red Eye jets swooped towards the Rhino. "You've got to take them out!"

Casey hunkered down in the turret and lined up her shot. The Phantoms were flying fast. She knew from years of playing video games that she would have to lead them a little, positioning the gun's target slightly ahead of the moving ships to make up for their speed. Frowning in concentration, she pressed the trigger. It was stiff and heavy, and it took her longer to pull back than she expected. The rail gun hummed, power building, and then spat out a round of electrified plasma. The Phantom's pilots peeled off left and right, their ships' wings tilting vertically as they dodged her shot.

Casey cursed. The delay on the trigger pull had messed up her aim. She wanted to regain that feeling of intense concentration she'd had in the shopping centre earlier that afternoon, but it didn't seem to come. Surely this was exactly like a video game? Racing along in a truck, while shooting from a gun turret at attacking jets. She'd played levels like this in so many games. She just needed to focus. What had her dad told her?

Go with the flow.

Easier said than done, especially when you were here in real life, buffeted by gunfire, explosions and a rising sense of dread that wrapped itself tight around your spine like a boa constrictor.

The Phantoms came around for another attack run, approaching the Rhino from behind this time. Casey's heart hammered in her ears; her hands trembled on the rail gun. She felt overwhelmed by fear.

Breathe, she told herself. She remembered all the sniper games she'd ever played. The ones where you had to steel yourself before taking an important shot, rather than just blasting wildly. They were all about staying in control, calming your avatar's heart rate so you could focus. She took a deep breath of the beach air, then gently released it again.

A wave of calm washed over her. She lined up the lead Phantom in her sights. She had it bang on this time, her helmet display flashing at her to take the shot. Everything else around her seemed to fall away.

This was it. She was in the moment. In full flow.

Her finger tightened on the trigger. Ready for its heavy pull this time.

Then it happened again.

Casey. We need your help.

The voice seemed to come from nowhere.

She felt the same strange presence sneak into her mind, rummaging through her thoughts. It was like a tentacle, probing and inquisitive.

Her hand froze on the rail gun. The Phantoms were coming in low and fast, right in the centre of her cone of fire. But she couldn't concentrate. Not with this stranger prowling around inside her head.

"Shoot, Casey!" Elite yelled over the comms. "They're right there!"

His voice seemed far, far away.

She tried to refocus and pull the trigger.

You have to come to us, the voice said.

Casey tried to push the voice away again. Whoever was speaking to her seemed oblivious to the danger she was in.

"Take the shot!" the boys shouted over the comms. "Now!"

She felt her finger pull on the trigger. The rail gun fired twice. Two bursts of plasma streaked through the sky towards the Phantoms …

… and missed them both!

Casey stared, unable to believe what she was seeing. She only had a split second to duck down into the turret as the attack ships strafed the Rhino with their cannons, hammering the rear of the vehicle.

Elite swerved to avoid the worst of it and the Rhino lurched into a side wheelie, almost toppling over. Casey, shaken around in the turret like a ragdoll, felt the presence in her mind evaporate and retreat.

"Casey?" Cheeze said urgently. "Can you hear us? Are you hurt?"

"I'm… I'm OK." She swung the gun around, readying for the Phantom's next pass.

"How could you miss?" Fish demanded over the comms. "They were right in front of you. It was a total gift!"

"I don't know. Something happened. I choked…"

The silence on the comms stung her more than any rebuke. She knew she'd let her teammates down. She wanted to tell them about the strange presence in her head. But they'd probably think she was crazy and, even if she dared, there wasn't time.

A crackle of static burst over the comms.

"They're coming back!" Elite shouted.

The Phantoms were streaking towards them again. Casey swung the gun around and lined up the first target. The ship bobbed from side to side, the pilot trying to throw off her aim. Its cannon fired, spitting out death. Casey didn't flinch. This time she was determined to make the shot. Her mind cleared as she focussed. She felt the rhythm of the ship's movement as if it was patched into her body.

Left. Right. Down. Lead it a little… *Now!*

The rail gun juddered and she watched her shot rip through the air. It hit the Phantom dead centre and a fireball erupted as the ship was blown out of the sky. The cockpit canopy flew off and the Red Eye pilot burst out, thrown upwards by his ejector seat, narrowly escaping being cooked alive in the explosion.

Casey didn't have time to celebrate before the second Phantom barrelled towards her from the other side, cutting across the Rhino's path. She desperately swung the gun onto it.

Too late! An alarm buzzed and her helmet display flashed red as the Phantom launched a heat-seeking sidewinder missile at them.

"Hold on!" Elite yelled on the comms. "I'll try and dodge it!" He swung the Rhino around. The missile followed them, relentless in its pursuit.

"I've got to shoot it down!" Casey shouted into her helmet mic.

"It's too close!" Elite replied. "You'll blow us up too!"

"We haven't got a choice!"

"I can shake it! Just give me a second."

Casey knew with every fibre of her being that Elite was wrong. The missile was bearing down on them, its sleek body cutting through the air like an arrow. It was so close now she could see the red marking along its flanks. There was no way Elite could avoid it.

She turned the turret around and forced the targeting system to track the missile instead of the Phantom. Her heads-up display flashed as the rail gun locked on. She curved her finger around the trigger. The missile, aware that it was being targeted, took evasive action.

Casey's eyes narrowed. She felt her body relax and her mind clear once more. She had been here before. She knew what to do. She let her instincts take over, forgetting all her doubts and fears as she felt herself totally in the zone. She didn't even rely on the targeting system, instead tracking the missile with her naked eyes as it came closer and closer and closer and …

FWHUMP!

The rail gun fired. A streak of hot green plasma, crackling with electrical charge, flew from its barrel. It tore towards the missile.

"Noooo!" Elite yelled over the comms.

Whatever he said next was swallowed by the blast as the missile exploded in mid-air just a couple of metres behind the Rhino. The blast threw the fleeing vehicle off the ground like a leaf in a hurricane and it flipped over once and then twice. Casey's harness ripped and she was thrown free of the turret. She hit the sand before she even had a chance to scream. Up ahead, the Rhino flipped one more time and then skidded on its side into a sand dune.

Casey lay on the beach, staring up at the two suns above her in a stunned daze. It struck her how far she was from home.

Then she passed out.

6

IS SHE ALWAYS THIS CRAZY, OR IS IT A NEW THING?

When he saw Casey lying on the beach, Pete thought his sister was dead. He'd crawled out of the wrecked Rhino, battered and bruised, behind the other boys, and stumbled to where Casey lay crumpled, grains of purple sand dancing over her face as they blew in off the sea. She had been thrown a couple of metres from the vehicle and she wasn't moving.

Pete was crowded out by the Ghost Reapers as they gathered around Casey. He felt small and useless, unable to remember any first aid. It wasn't until Brain, who played as the squad's medic, started shouting that they needed to get her to safety that Pete knew for sure she was still alive.

He looked on, scared and uncertain how to help. He knew he wasn't like Casey, fearless and heroic.

She was born for action. It was in her DNA. Their dad would have been proud of her. Pete wasn't sure what their dad would have made of him, though. He didn't seem to be good for anything except getting captured. He touched his dad's dog tags; the ones Casey had given him for luck before they dropped onto this alien planet. Right now, they felt more like a reprimand than a source of comfort. He wiped a film of sweat from his face, cursing the heat of the two suns.

As the boys lifted Casey between them, Pete bent down and picked up her helmet, forgotten on the sand. He tucked it under his arm. It didn't feel like much of a contribution to the rescue effort.

"We're heading to that bunker," Brain called out, signalling Pete to follow. Across the beach, Pete could see an abandoned Squid structure rising out of the sand. He hoped it was strong enough to protect them from the Phantom's guns. They were far behind the frontlines now and their stretch of the beach was quiet and still. The invading gamers had marched on ahead towards the cliffs, taking the conflict with them.

As the boys moved off carrying Casey, Pete suddenly remembered Xander. He looked around and saw the YouTuber crawling out of the wreckage of the Rhino.

"Hey! A little help over here…"

Pete rushed over. He grabbed the older boy and pulled him free. Xander looked shaken up by the crash, but Pete was glad to see the distant look in his eyes was gone.

"Thanks, kid. That's twice you've saved me now."

"Twice?" Pete asked, uncertain what the teenager meant.

"If it wasn't for you, I'd still be marching alongside the rest of those zombies," Xander said, pulling the busted Arcturian mind-control device off his head and wincing as it ripped free. He tossed it into the sand. Pete felt a warm glow of pride. At least someone thought he was useful. Then he glanced back towards the group carrying Casey and felt guilty. Now wasn't the time to be thinking about himself.

"Don't worry," Xander reassured him, following Pete's gaze, "your sister is one tough cookie." He paused, then added, "Is she always that reckless, though? She almost got us all killed on the Rhino. Who shoots a missile out of the air like that? It's a miracle we weren't blown up."

Pete looked at his sister, her face obscured by her blue-streaked hair as the boys carried her limp body. Had she saved them? Or had she just been reckless like Xander said? It was true, she could be impetuous. Like pretending to be a boy to the rest of her *SkyWake* team and then letting him take her place in the eSports tournament to save face. Or trying to single-handedly stop an alien invasion. Or—

A shout interrupted his thoughts. The fortified door of the bunker had slid open, and a man stood in the shadows gesturing towards them.

"Hurry! You'll be safe in here."

Pete recognized him instantly. "Lieutenant Dreyfus!"

The military officer from the shopping centre waved them inside impatiently, casting a careful glance around the beach to make sure they weren't spotted by any Red Eyes. His olive-green polo shirt and khaki cargo trousers were dusty from the sand. He must have been surviving on his own since they hot-dropped onto the beach.

Pete was the last one inside. Just before the doors closed, he caught sight of the Phantom flying across the beach, buzzing over the wreckage of the Rhino as it searched for the survivors. He was glad when the bunker doors locked behind them.

The inside of the bunker was dark and shadowy. The internal lights had been blown out in an earlier firefight and the air was tinged with the smell of burning electrics. An automated cannon sat on a tripod, poking through a window slit that looked out onto the beach. Its control panel smoked, useless. Crates of equipment were stacked against the far wall. There were no Squids or Red Eyes to be seen anywhere, dead or alive.

Pete noticed a huge hatch in the floor. He guessed it led down to the tunnels that ran under the beach, just like in *SkyWake*. It was sealed tight. But that didn't stop him from shivering as he remembered the Squid they'd seen emerge from the sand back in the crater. He'd always hated the Bactu, even when they were just enemies on Casey's monitor back home. There was something about their tentacles and their ancient, knowing eyes that made him shudder.

"Lay her down gently," Dreyfus instructed the Reapers as they brought Casey inside. "Support her neck."

Once Casey was on the floor, the military man checked her vitals and grunted.

"Will she be OK?" Pete asked, hovering at his shoulder, unable to read Dreyfus's craggy face.

"It's a miracle she's still breathing," the soldier told him. "I saw it all from here. That explosion threw her right out of the turret." He ran his hand over Casey's exo-suit. "This alien technology must be incredibly advanced. She couldn't have survived a blast like that without it."

"But will she be all right?" Pete demanded, his heart thumping.

Brain pulled his med tool from his utility belt and stared at it thoughtfully. It looked like a handheld supermarket scanner. "If we were in the game, I'd just heal her up with this."

"You can't use that thing on my sister!"

"Yeah, bruv," Elite agreed. "It's designed for Red Eyes. Who knows what their insides are like? They could have three hearts or anything."

"If the Red Eyes gave these to the gamers, they must have some value," Brain suggested.

"When you get blown up, you can try it on yourself," Cheeze said firmly. "Until then, back off." He knelt beside Casey, his power suit whirring as he bent down and squeezed her hand. "She's gonna be fine. Aren't you, Casey?"

She didn't respond.

Pete saw Brain and Fish exchange a worried glance.

"She'll live," Dreyfus reassured them. "But she'll have a hell of a headache when she wakes up."

Xander cleared his throat and stepped forward.

"Look, I don't want to talk out of turn here, but you guys should probably think about promoting someone else to run your squad. Casey's taken a hell of a beating and if we're gonna get off this alien planet and find a way back home, we need someone to take charge. The lieutenant can't do it – he doesn't know enough about *SkyWake*. We need someone who knows the game inside out."

"Someone like you, you mean?" Cheeze demanded, annoyed. He clearly didn't have much love for Xander.

The YouTuber held his palms up and took a step backwards. "Whoa, dude. Calm down. I didn't mean me. I meant him." He tossed his fringe out of his eyes and pointed at Brain. "You're the eldest, right?" he said. "You're definitely the smartest. You must be the Ghost Reapers' second in command."

"We've never had a second in command," Brain said. He looked flattered by the attention.

"Seriously?" Xander asked, surprised. "Well, that's a rookie mistake. All the pro teams have one. It's the only way to play a game like *SkyWake*. You need a proper chain of command in case the team leader hits the game-over screen." He looked at Dreyfus, as if seeking his approval. "That's what real soldiers do, right, Lieutenant?"

Dreyfus grunted. Pete guessed he didn't like Xander either. But then, he didn't seem to like anyone much. The Reapers looked at one another uncomfortably. None of them wanted to be the first to suggest themselves as replacement.

"Casey'll be fine," Cheeze said. "She just needs a minute to catch her breath. She's unstoppable. Right, Pete?"

Pete shifted his weight from one foot to another. He wasn't sure what he was supposed to say. She looked pretty stopped to him.

"Even if she is fine, what then?" Xander asked. "Are you sure she even knows what she's doing? She almost got us killed out there."

"She's got us this far," Fish said defensively. "She got us off the dropship. I reckoned we were all goners for sure."

"Yeah, but she thought we were in orbit over Earth," Elite muttered. "Ending up on Hosin was not what I signed up for."

Fish gave his friend a disappointed stare.

"What?" Elite shrugged. "I'm just telling it like it is."

"She rescued me," said Pete, remembering how his sister had come after him in the middle of all the chaos in the shopping centre.

"Exactly," Xander said, clapping him on the shoulder. "And she almost got us all killed doing it. What I'm saying is, she's been through a lot and maybe her judgement isn't what it was. She's making bad calls." He looked at Casey's teammates, almost challenging them to argue with him. Pete guessed he was doing some sort of mental jiu-jitsu – agreeing with the boys to make them disagree with one another.

"We've *all* been through a lot," Cheeze snapped, tapping his power suit. "The Red Eyes destroyed my wheelchair and now I have to wear this thing. Do you have any idea how much it hurts?"

"Yeah, but ever since we got to Hosin, Casey's been…" Elite let his voice trail off.

"Go on," Cheeze said, glaring at him. "Finish your sentence."

"Well, what I'm saying is, like… She ain't been right. She froze up on the Rhino. She could have taken those Phantoms out, but she choked. Then she blew us up by shooting the missile when it was too close. I ain't dissing her, but…"

"Maybe it's too much for her," Brain suggested.

"Reality check!" Cheeze spat angrily. "We are on an alien planet in the middle of a war we've only ever seen in a video game. It's too much for all of us."

Brain tutted. "You're being too emotional."

Cheeze stood up, his Red Eye power suit jerking unsteadily as it took the strain. Pete noticed him wince. The suit didn't seem to be working properly. Maybe that was why he was so annoyed. "Casey gets my vote," he said. "She's our shot caller. Always has been, always will be. Who's with me?"

"Keep your voice down, son," Dreyfus warned. "We're in enemy territory here."

Xander turned to Pete. "What's your take on all this? You're her brother. You know her better than anyone. How can we help her?"

Pete chewed his lip uncertainly. He didn't like arguments like this.

"You can't ask him to be judge and jury on his own sister," said Brain.

"He's a smart kid. I've seen him in action. He's got a lot of heart." Xander tapped his chest and winked at Pete. "We're all just trying to do the best thing for your sister. What do you think? Should someone else lead for a while? Maybe she can take back the reins when she's feeling herself again?"

Pete hesitated. Xander made it sound so reasonable. He'd seen how distracted Casey had been on the Rhino and how she had choked when they needed her most. Something was wrong, but he wasn't sure what. Maybe it *was* too much for her. Maybe she was just as scared as he was. If someone took over for her, it might let her catch her breath. Like a tag team in a wrestling match. No one would be replacing her, they'd just be helping her.

He realized everyone was waiting for him. He gathered his scattered thoughts and swallowed hard, determined to do this right for once. He'd blow them away by laying out the pros and cons. He'd be the one to guide them towards the right decision. This was his moment to shine.

"Go on, Pete," Xander encouraged. "Tell us what you think. We're all listening."

Pete cleared his throat. Then another voice spoke up from across the bunker.

"I'll tell you what *I* think..." Casey said groggily, pulling herself upright.

Pete's words died on his lips.

7

IF YOU DON'T KNOW
WHAT A TROLLEY IS,
THAT'S A PROBLEM

Casey pulled herself up off the floor, every muscle in her body aching. Black bruises were already forming on her forearms and her back felt sore when she moved.

"Casey! You scared the hell out of us!" Cheeze cried, helping her back onto her feet.

"How did we get inside a Squid bunker?" she mumbled, looking around. "Last thing I remember, I was in the turret…" She caught sight of Dreyfus in the shadows on the edge of the group. He gave her a gruff nod.

"Are you OK?" Pete asked, running over and giving her a hug that made her wince. She tried not to push him off.

"What's going on?" she asked. "Are you voting on who should replace me?" She meant it as a joke, but she couldn't help but notice the guilty look that spread over the boys' faces.

"That's right," Xander said, with no trace of shame. "We're worried about you. We were asking Pete who he thought should step up to take your place."

"No one is replacing Casey!" Cheeze interrupted. "Are they?" he added, turning to his teammates. The boys stared intently at their feet as if someone was projecting a sneak preview of the latest Marvel movie down there.

"It's OK," Casey said. "I never asked to be in charge. I never even wanted to be leader." She was too tired and sore to argue.

"What happened back on the Rhino?" Brain asked. "You froze up." His tone was more curious than accusatory.

"I don't know," Casey admitted. She paused, uncertain whether she should tell them the truth or not. "It was like something reached out to me. I heard this voice in my head telling me not be afraid and…" Her words trailed off.

Brain's expression was doubtful. "Who do you think it was?"

Casey kept her voice level. "I think it was the Bactu."

Nobody said anything. "I think they want to help us," she continued, figuring she might as well get it all out. If the boys thought she was crazy, too bad. "That's why that Squid burst out of the crater even though we were miles from the front line. It came to save us from Scratch."

"Maybe they know we're not the enemy," Cheeze suggested. He looked at Brain, hoping for back-up, but the boy simply stood there, deep in thought.

"I played as the Squids in *SkyWake*," Xander said. "I know what they're like. They don't help nobody, never. They're evil."

"Yeah," Fish agreed, glancing nervously at the hatch in the floor. "They're the bad guys. All slithering and slimy and—"

"Who says they're the bad guys?" Cheeze asked. "Just because you saw it in the game doesn't mean it's true. If the Red Eyes made *SkyWake*, of course they'd say the Squids were evil."

"True dat," Elite agreed, leaning on his sniper rifle. "It's like … propaganda, innit?"

"You're missing the bigger picture here," Xander told them, impatiently. "We're in the middle of an alien war that's got nothing to do with us. We don't need to take sides. But the only people who can get us home are the Red Eyes. I'm not saying we should be besties with the Arcturians, but we can't go chasing after the Squids just because Casey heard a..." He paused. "What was it again?"

"A voice," Cheeze said, finishing Xander's sentence on Casey's behalf. "She called it a voice."

Xander let the word hang in the air a moment, watching the rest of the Ghost Reapers' faces.

"We think you need to take a break," he told Casey. "You're not Supergirl."

"I'm just trying to get everyone home safely," she said, defensively. She didn't like the way Xander used "we", as if he was talking for the whole group. There was something hard-nosed and manipulative about him. Maybe you didn't become a social media influencer with a million subscribers without a ruthless streak.

She felt the boys' support for her wavering. Perhaps Xander was right. Perhaps she *was* losing it. She glanced at Pete, but he couldn't look her in the eye. She realized her brother had lost faith in her too. That hit harder than anything.

"If the Squids are trying to reach out to us, we need to find out what they want," she said.

"How?" Elite demanded. "By going into the tunnels and asking them?" He looked over at the floor hatch. "I hate enclosed spaces. But I hate enclosed spaces with creepy, tentacled aliens in them even more."

"If we're going to turn off the signal that's controlling the gamers, the Squids can't help us with that," Brain said.

"Then we should stay on the beach," Xander said. He flicked his fringe out of his eyes as if that was the end of the matter. Casey's aching body sagged. She felt she'd just lost a game she hadn't even realized she was playing.

The Reapers rested in the bunker for almost an hour, listening to the battle unfolding on the beach outside. As the others sat around comparing bruises and wishing they had something to eat, Elite took a pencil and notebook from his pocket and scribbled in it, rapping under his breath as he tried to come up with some new rhymes.

"Do you have to do that?" Brain demanded.

"It calms me down." He twiddled the pencil around in his fingers. "I need a word to make this work. What rhymes with 'existence'?"

"'Distance'," Brain said, immediately rising to the challenge.

"Sweet!"

Casey limped over to the bunker's narrow firing slits and looked out onto the beach. More Phantoms streaked across the sky and heavy explosions thudded in the distance as they launched their rockets at the Squids' clifftop base. It didn't seem as though the Squid had any aircraft to fight back with. In fact, they didn't appear to have much of anything. All they seemed to do was fire their artillery. It was like they didn't want to engage the invaders head on.

Maybe, Casey thought to herself, they were waiting for the gamers to reach the base and head into the tunnels beneath it. Despite their nickname, the squid-like Bactu didn't live in water. Their home was a network of caverns beneath the planet's surface. In the close confines underground, they could dominate the attacking forces, blitzing them with their psychic powers like Mind Control, Psi-Blast and Telekinesis. At least, that was how it was in the game.

She was deep in thought when Dreyfus appeared beside her.

He gazed out at the beach, appraising the carnage with a veteran's eye.

"It's unlike any battle I've ever seen," he admitted, "and I served in both Iraq and Afghanistan."

Casey still hadn't got used to Dreyfus being part of the team. In the shopping mall it had felt like he was her enemy. Since their escape, though, he'd treated her like an equal. She had clearly impressed him with her skill with the Arcturian plasma rifle and her ability to lead the boys. But now... Well, now it felt like everything was falling apart. They were light years away from Earth with no hope of getting back. She didn't want to be in charge. She just wanted to be at home watching *The X-Factor* with her mum and Pete like she should be doing on a Saturday night.

"It's hard, being a leader," Dreyfus said, as if guessing her thoughts. "People think it's a popularity contest, but it's not. It's about making decisions and taking responsibility for them. Because sooner or later, you're going to be faced with a situation where there is no good choice."

"What do you mean?"

Dreyfus straightened his back a little. "Have you ever heard of the trolley problem?"

Casey shook her head.

"It's a famous thought experiment about a runaway tram, what our American cousins used to call a 'trolley'. Imagine that there's a tram racing down the tracks, out of control. It's heading towards five unsuspecting workers who are on the tramline up ahead. There's nothing anyone can do to stop it crashing into them, except you. You're standing next to a control switch. If you pull it, you'll be able to divert the tram onto another track where there's only one worker. So, the question is: do you change the path of the tram and kill one person to save five? Or do you do nothing and let five people die?"

Casey sucked her teeth, thinking. "I guess saving five people has to be better than saving one, doesn't it?" she said, then hesitated. "I'm not sure I'd want to kill that one worker, though. I mean, if I do nothing, they'll live. Why should I be the one to decide that they should die, just to save the others?"

"If you don't pull the switch, though, five people will be killed."

"But if I do pull it, I'll kill someone who would have survived. It'd be on me. I'd have to live with it for ever."

Dreyfus nodded. "It gets even harder if you imagine that single worker is someone you know. Your best friend, or someone in your family. Suddenly it becomes personal. Although the logic of losing one person to save five stays the same, it makes it a lot harder to choose to sacrifice them."

"So, what's the right answer?" Casey asked.

"There isn't one," the soldier grunted. "That's the point. There's no good choice because there's no way to save everyone. You just have to choose the least bad outcome."

Casey frowned. "Have you ever had to make a choice like that, Lieutenant?"

Dreyfus fell silent a moment and stared out at the beach, then nodded. "Many years ago, when I was serving in Iraq. My unit was in the mountains visiting some local tribal leaders when we were ambushed by an enemy we'd never encountered before." His eyes narrowed as if he was replaying the events somewhere deep inside his head. "They came out of nowhere. They wore armour that was impervious to our bullets, and they carried strange but deadly weapons; we didn't stand a chance."

Casey gasped as she realized who he was talking about.

"The Red Eyes?"

"I took a blast from one of their weapons," he said and his hand involuntarily reached to the purple plasma scar that sneaked out from under his polo shirt. "Lying there in the dirt, left for dead, I watched them massacre my squad. The only person they spared was my radio operator, Private Ross. He was just a kid.

Barely eighteen and on his first tour. The lads in the squad used to call him 'Pac-Man' because he was mad about video games. As I watched them drag him onto their spaceship, I realized I had a choice. I could try and fight back, even though I knew it would be suicide; or I could pretend to be dead and survive to tell my superiors what had happened."

Casey saw the pain of that decision on the lieutenant's granite face.

"We think that was the first time the Red Eyes came to Earth. They made a few more incursions over the years, always in war zones. It was like they were testing our military ability. A little later, the top brass put together a secret NATO team called EXDEF – the Extraterrestrial Defence Force. They put me in charge of it, and it was our job to monitor for future alien attacks. I hoped that one day, I'd be able to find Private Ross and bring him home."

"You should have tried to stop them from taking him prisoner," Casey said, and immediately felt guilty. It wasn't her place to judge. To her surprise, though, Dreyfus didn't get angry.

"You're right," he said. "But you're also wrong. If I'd fought them, I would have died, and no one would have survived to warn people about the Red

Eyes. I went with my gut and now I live with the consequences." He let his voice drop low. "A day hasn't gone by without me thinking about that kid. 'Leave no man behind' is the military's creed. But I did exactly that."

Casey felt sorry for him. He made her think of her dad. She wondered what the two soldiers would have said to each other if they could have met. Would her dad have had a solution to the trolley problem? Would he have fought back against the Red Eyes or sacrificed a soldier for the greater good? She didn't know.

Casey was about to say something more when a movement caught her eye across the beach. Two squads of Red Eyes led by Scratch were moving slowly but surely across the sand towards the bunker.

"Oh no," she gulped. "They've found us."

8

YOU CAN RUN OR YOU CAN JUMP, BUT YOU CAN'T DO BOTH

The Red Eyes approached the bunker cautiously, fanning out across the rolling sand dunes that lay on either side of it. A gentle breeze blew in off the sea, offering some welcome respite as it stirred the humid air. The aliens moved in tight squads, covering one another as they advanced. It meant their progress was slow, but it was the safest way to advance on a fortified bunker.

"Doesn't she ever give up?" Casey asked, watching Scratch through the firing slit. The alien's reptilian features were pinched with anger.

"She's not going to stop until she's got revenge," Dreyfus replied, putting a hand on Casey's shoulder. "It's personal between you two now."

Casey shuddered, aware how true that was. She'd made an enemy. One who wanted to destroy her. The boys looked as glum as she felt, clearly realizing how much danger they were in.

"We need to get out of here," Xander said. "If we move quickly, we can put some distance between us and them."

"We can't keep running," Cheeze said wearily. "*I* definitely can't. Not in this suit. It's barely working any more."

"If we stay here, we're gonna be overrun," said Elite. "The bunker's automated plasma cannons are offline. We can't hold them back."

"What would we do if this was a *SkyWake* game?" Brain asked.

"I'd be hitting Alt+F4 right about now," Fish muttered. "Then I'd go and play some *Animal Crossing* on the Switch. Do some fishing. Get some Nook Miles. De-stress." He let out a sigh, imagining himself back home.

"In our final match of the tournament, we all went underground," Casey said, remembering how they'd gone into the tunnels under the beach during the match against Xander's team at the shopping centre.

"Yeah, and the Squids found us and fried us," Elite replied.

"But what if they're trying to help us now?" Casey asked.

Xander shook his head. "You're wrong, Casey. The Squids are not your friends. If you take everyone into the tunnels, you'll never make it back out again."

"Well, they're the only aliens we've met so far who haven't tried to abduct us, kill us or mind-control us," she snapped. "I say we go into the tunnels and take our chances." She looked at Pete and signalled him to join her. He didn't move.

"No way," Elite said forcefully. "Not doing it. Not happening. Next idea."

"You really think the Squids are trying to help us?" Cheeze asked her.

"Yes," she replied firmly, although in her heart she wasn't as certain as she sounded. She hoped her hunch was right. She looked at the boys, sensing their scepticism.

"I don't think we should make tactical decisions based on a voice you heard after hitting your head," Xander said.

"True dat," Elite agreed, nodding. "Concussion can make you go funny."

"You just don't want to go into the tunnels because you're scared of small spaces," Cheeze snapped. Elite looked hurt and Cheeze regretted his words instantly. "I'm sorry," he muttered. "I didn't mean—"

"Let's vote," Xander interrupted. He watched the Red Eyes' progress. They were still a few minutes away.

"OK," Casey said. "Who wants the beach?"

Brain and Elite raised their hands. Xander too. Casey saw Pete hesitate for a moment, his hand twitching, but he didn't raise it. She felt a jolt of relief.

"And who wants to head into the tunnels?" she asked.

Casey raised her hand. Cheeze did the same. Fish *umm*-ed and *ahh*-ed, his face frowning and uncertain. Elite watched his friend expectantly and then sighed in exasperation when Fish raised his hand to support Casey.

"Aw, c'mon," the sniper said, shaking his head in disbelief.

"She's got us this far," said the Scottish boy defensively. "I believe in her."

"Thanks, Fish." Casey turned to Dreyfus. "Lieutenant?"

"I'm not voting," Dreyfus said. "I've never played *SkyWake*. I don't know enough about any of this to make a decision. I'll go with whatever the majority decides."

That left only one person. "You're the deciding vote, little brother," said Casey.

Pete shrank back as everyone turned to look at him. "I can't..." he said, shaking his head.

"Just choose whatever you think is best," Casey explained. "Beach or tunnels?" Casey glanced quickly through the slit at the approaching Red Eyes. "But you need to hurry."

"You're pressuring him," Xander complained.

"Because we're running out of time!"

"I vote for the beach," Pete said quietly.

Casey stared at him. His cheeks burned crimson.

"I'm sorry, Casey," he said. "But I think you're wrong. Whatever's happening with the Squids is a trap. If you weren't so exhausted, you might see that too."

Casey felt as if she'd been punched in the chest.

"But the Squids reached out to me," she said, unable to see why he didn't believe her. "They need our help ... and they want to help us in return."

"You don't know that," Pete snapped. "Not for sure."

"So, that's it, then," Xander said, not quite able to hide his smile. "We'll escape onto the beach. Majority rules."

"Maybe we should just split up," Casey suggested.

She felt sulky and petulant. "The Squids asked me to help them. I can't just ignore that."

"No," Fish said firmly. "I play D&D, and the one thing I've learned – apart from that rogues will always rob your backpack when you sleep – is that you should *never* split the party. We have to—"

A barrage of plasma fire raked the bunker, interrupting him in mid-sentence.

"They're here!" Dreyfus shouted, pushing the boys away from the firing slits.

"Get into the tunnels!" Casey shouted.

"No! Get onto the beach," Xander commanded. "If we go out the rear doors, the bunker will give us some cover."

There was a clatter as a Red Eye grunt dropped several objects, smooth as cobblestones, into the bunker through the firing slit. As they hit the ground, they sprouted spindly legs and click-clacked into life.

"Tarantulas!" Casey yelled, recognizing the robot-spiders instantly. She blasted at a couple with her plasma rifle, but they jumped out of her way and the shots merely scorched the bunker floor. Chaos erupted as everyone ran in different directions.

"Don't split the party!" Fish yelled, but his voice was drowned out by plasma fire.

Casey retreated towards the hatch that led to the tunnels, blasting at the tarantulas as they scurried across the floor and up the walls. Cheeze was already there, hacking into the hatch's control panel.

"It's open!" he shouted as the doors in the floor slid back to reveal a deep black hole. Before Casey could stop him, he jumped straight into it, vanishing into the darkness. Casey turned and blasted a tarantula that was leaping at Brain. It exploded into fragments. Then she hurried over to the hatch and looked down it. There wasn't a ladder, just a sheer drop into the blackness below.

"Cheeze?" she yelled. "Cheeze! Are you OK?"

There was no answer. She hesitated on the edge of the drop, feeling that same alien presence creeping into her head. Encouraging her on.

Jump, Casey.

She stared into the hole, wondering how deep it was. She still couldn't see Cheeze. More plasma fire burst around her as the Red Eyes reached the front of the bunker and blindly fired in through the slits.

Trust us.

Casey dropped into the darkness and tried not to scream.

9

LIGHT AT THE END OF THE TUNNEL, OR JUST A SPEEDING TRAIN COMING TOWARDS US?

It was so dark in the tunnel beneath the bunker that Casey couldn't even see her own hand in front of her face. In the absence of sight, the first thing she noticed was the smell. The tunnels were dank and damp with the musty aroma of an old basement. She reached out to touch the tunnel wall and shuddered, disgusted. It was coated in a sticky substance that bound itself to her fingers like glue.

She fumbled for the torch on the side of her helmet. Its beam cut through the darkness, glittering across the slime-coated walls. She saw Cheeze in the gloom. He was shaken from the fall, but gave her a weak thumbs up as her torch dazzled his eyes.

There was a yelp behind them as Fish landed in

the tunnel with a heavy thud. A second later, Dreyfus dropped down beside him with perfect poise.

"Worst funfair ride *ever*," the Scottish boy muttered as he regained his footing. A burst of plasma fire echoed in the bunker above.

"Where are the others?" Casey asked.

"We're it," Fish said. "Everyone else ran for the exit."

"Pete?"

"With Xander. I'm sorry."

A tarantula appeared on the lip of the hatch above. It paused, staring down at them with its beady, robotic eyes. Cheeze hit the control panel on the tunnel wall and the hatch slid shut. The tarantula, too slow to react, got one of its legs caught in the hatch as it closed. The severed metal limb dropped into the tunnel, thrashing like a landed fish on the deck of a boat. Casey crunched her boot down on it angrily. It sparked and fell still.

"I can't believe Pete chose Xander over me."

"It was chaos up there," Fish said, struggling to turn his torch on. He thumped the side of his helmet until it flickered into life. "He probably didn't have a choice."

Casey didn't respond.

"What do we do now?" Dreyfus asked. "Where do these tunnels go?"

Casey looked out into the darkness. The beam of her helmet torch was swallowed up by the inky blackness.

"I guess there's only one way to find out," she said and marched off. Fish and Cheeze shrugged at one another in the weak light of their own torches and then followed, doing their best not to touch the sticky walls. Dreyfus stayed in the rear, keeping his plasma pistol at the ready.

The tunnel system was a labyrinth, with endless shafts leading off the main route. Some were sealed by heavy metal doors while others simply stretched off into darkness, heading who knew where. Fish and Cheeze tried to keep count of them all, but they soon lost track. Only Casey seemed unfazed. She marched ahead, turning left and right as if she was following some memorized route.

"How does she know where she's going?" Fish asked, slowing down a little to let Cheeze catch up.

"Search me," Cheeze said testily. His power suit seemed to be functioning worse since the fall, jerking and stuttering as he forced it to move his legs for him.

Fish noticed his friend's discomfort with concern. "That suit's really hurting you, isn't it?"

"It's killing me. I normally spend all day in my

wheelchair. My body's not used to being upright like this. I thought the suit would fix everything, but it's not supposed to be a mobility aid and my nervous system is rejecting the link. I just want to get rid of it."

"Lean on me a bit."

"No way!" Cheeze said, embarrassed. Fish ignored his protests and pulled Cheeze's arm around his shoulder, taking some of his weight.

"I've got you, buddy. Don't be shy." Their faces were practically cheek to cheek like ballroom dancers doing a tango. "Just pretend we're in a three-legged race at sports day."

"I've missed a lot of things since I got my wheelchair, but the three-legged race isn't one of them."

"Shh!" Casey warned. She paused and stared into the darkness. The tunnel ahead split three ways, each as dark as the others. "Something's coming."

The boys and the lieutenant held their breath and peered into the gloom over her shoulder.

"I can't hear anything," Fish said, squinting. He shifted his weight better to support Cheeze, then took his shield baton in his free hand, ready to extend the energy barrier around them if they came under attack. Cheeze brought his plasma rifle up, holding it with one hand as he clung to Fish with the other. Behind them, Dreyfus gripped his plasma pistol, ready to fire at anything that came from the rear.

They waited.

Nothing happened.

"Is it the Squids?" Fish asked. His helmet torch flickered off and on again. "My battery's almost dead." He thumped it and, after one last flicker, it went out for good. "Oh, that's just great."

Casey put her hand in the air for silence. She felt the same presence creeping into her mind. Her muscles tightened in anticipation, although she couldn't say what, exactly, she was waiting for.

Don't be afraid, the voice said.

"Casey!" Cheeze shouted at her, unable to understand why she seemed to have frozen. "Tell us what to—"

A noise from the tunnel silenced him: a gathering rush, like wind howling. A moment later, they all felt the ground and the walls start to vibrate. Something big was moving towards them and it was coming at speed.

"What is that?" Fish asked, his voice quivering.

The Squid ripped through the darkness, its huge head bobbing up and down as it flew along the tunnel like an express train. It propelled itself using its tentacles, whipping them underneath its body and along the sides of the tunnel in a furious, threshing motion. This was why the tunnels were covered in slime, Casey realized. The Squids secreted it as they moved, using it to lubricate their path.

A moment later, she heard a similar sound coming from other tunnels – including the one they had just come down. The Squids were homing in on their position.

"Contact rear!" Dreyfus shouted as a Squid burst out of the darkness behind them. He raised his pistol, keenly aware that such a little gun would be of no use against this enormous alien.

"We're surrounded," Fish yelled. His shield was up, but it could only cover one side at a time. He spun around trying to work out which way to face.

We're not here to hurt you.

It sounded like several voices all talking at once, one overlaid over the other. A whispering echo that reverberated through Casey's mind.

"They say they won't hurt us," she said aloud.

"And you believe them?" Fish asked, shuddering at the sight of these nightmarish creatures, which had now come to a stop in a circle around the group.

"Just don't do anything to provoke them," Casey

said. Then, taking a deep breath, she stepped through Fish's shield. The wall of light crackled around her and re-formed as she passed through.

"No, Casey! Don't!" Cheeze yelled.

The closest Squid moved forward, as if sensing how vulnerable Casey was outside the shield's protection. Casey pressed a couple of buttons on the side of her plasma rifle and cradled it in her arms.

"She's going to shake 'n' bake them," Cheeze murmured, remembering the tactic Casey had used in Starbucks to turn her rifle into a makeshift bomb.

"Yeah! Take 'em down, Casey!" Fish hollered excitedly, gripping his shield baton in readiness of the explosion. "Go with the flow!"

But Casey didn't go with the flow.

Instead, she stood completely still. The huge creature, as if surprised by her fearlessness, halted in front of her. Casey and the alien stared at each other for a moment. She looked into its rheumy eyes. They were deep and ancient and impossible to read.

The voice in her head had fallen silent, although she could feel the same presence skirting the edge of her mind like a burglar looking for a way inside.

She dropped to one knee and placed the plasma rifle on the ground like some kind of offering. The boys gasped. She hadn't set the gun to explode. She had simply deactivated it. The weapon lay on the floor of the tunnel, powered down and useless.

Fish looked at Cheeze in shock. "She's surrendering?"

Casey stood back up, her hands now empty, and stared at the Squid. Its massive body filled the whole tunnel. Its eyes were fixed on her, strange and alien. Then, after a moment or two, it reached out a tentacle. The tip, flatter and wider than the rest of the tentacle, hovered in front of her face. She could see the suckers on its underside, which seemed to twist and wriggle like sea anemones in the tide. She wanted to flee from this monstrous creature, but she forced herself to remain still.

The tentacle paused, as if giving her the opportunity to change her mind. Then it darted forward. She felt the suckers attach to her skin. The tentacle covered her eyes, nose and mouth, and it felt like a damp cloth pressed against her face. She started to lose consciousness. The last thing she heard were the panicked shouts of Dreyfus and the boys as the Squids surrounded them. She prayed that her friends wouldn't start shooting.

10

WINNER, WINNER, CHICKEN DINNER

Pete ran out of the bunker and across the beach, away from the Red Eyes and their tarantulas. The sand shimmered like a mirage in the heat. He didn't know where he was going: he was just blindly following Xander towards an outcrop of shiny black rocks. Clumps of spiky, striped vegetation rose up between them like cacti in a desert.

Just as they reached the outcrop, two sentry turrets emerged from the sand.

"Get down!" Xander shouted, pulling Pete onto his belly as the turrets began to scan for targets. They stayed low and crawled behind the safety of the rocks.

"If they start firing, they'll give away our position," Brain panted, crashing down beside them with Elite in tow.

Pete looked around. The four boys were lying in the middle of the rock formation, sheltered on all sides but no more than a hundred metres from the bunker. The rocks, black and shiny like polished onyx gemstones, gave them some cover. If they tried to make a run for it, though, they'd either be shot by the turrets or spotted by Scratch and the Red Eyes. The only thing they could do was stay low and pray no one searched in this direction.

Rolling onto his back, Pete stared up at the two suns. He didn't regret not going with Casey, although he hoped fervently that she had escaped. The thought of being trapped in the underground tunnels with the Squids made him shiver. He'd rather take his chances out here in the open. Maybe Xander was right: maybe Casey wasn't thinking clearly. After all, every *SkyWake* player knew that the tunnels were a death trap.

"What do we do now?" Elite asked, scanning the bunker through his sniper scope.

"I reckon we get out to sea," Xander said, looking towards the breaking waves. "Get a boat. Find an island. We could hide out like Robinson Crusoe."

"That's not a plan, it's a daydream," Brain replied sharply. "We've got no idea what the water is like. It could be toxic to humans. What lives in it? Sharks? Aliens?"

"Or maybe alien sharks…" Elite chipped in.

The YouTuber's face flashed with annoyance. "So, what do you want to do instead? Wait here and build sandcastles? Why don't you ask the Red Eyes if they brought buckets and spades?"

"We need to shut down the signal the Red Eyes are using to control the other gamers," Brain said. "It's the only way to rescue them."

"I'm more worried about us saving ourselves," Xander said.

Elite was outraged. "But your team's out there!"

Xander rolled his eyes. "Not my fault those idiots were dumb enough to get captured."

Brain pulled his glasses off and wiped them on his T-shirt. One of the lenses had cracked during the attack in the bunker and he had to squint to see through it properly. "I suggest we head up to the front lines and find a Red Eye overseer," he said. "Maybe they're the ones in charge of the signal."

Xander pulled himself into a crouch and spat onto the sand. "Go on then. Take your sniper and hop it. Me and the kid are gonna get off this beach and back to Earth." He glanced around the side of the rocks, eyeing the turrets. They were still scanning for targets.

"How?" Elite demanded.

"Winners always find a way." He looked at Pete. "Don't we?"

Before Pete could answer, a shadow fell over them.

"Not today," said a clunky AI voice as it translated the words from Arcturian into English. Scratch and her squad stood on the rocks looking down at the group. The four boys had been so busy arguing, they hadn't noticed the Red Eyes approach.

"Some leader," Elite told Xander as he dropped his sniper rifle into the sand. "We barely made it a hundred metres. We should've stayed with Casey."

"Cay See?" Scratch demanded. "Where is she?"

Xander opened his mouth to speak, but Brain cut him off. "Gone. The Squids took her into the tunnels."

Scratch hissed in anger. "Kill them," she ordered. There was a rattle of hardware as the Red Eyes raised their plasma rifles.

Please let it be painless, Pete thought. He closed his eyes and felt the fierce heat of the two suns on his face. What a way to die. Marooned on an alien planet.

"Wait!" Xander yelled. "I can get you what you want."

Pete opened his eyes a crack.

"What do you think I want?" Scratch asked, annoyed but a little intrigued.

"Casey… I can help you find her."

"How?"

Pete looked at the arrogant YouTuber in panic, wondering what on earth he was going to say next.

"This," Xander said, snaking his arm around Pete's shoulder, "is her brother."

Scratch's eyes blinked as the words were translated. Not an ordinary blink, up and down, but a sideways, lizard blink that made Pete's stomach churn.

"Why did you tell them that?" the frightened boy asked.

"Trust me," the YouTuber whispered back. "It's for the win."

A dropship was waiting for them by the time they reached the shoreline, its landing gear submerged in the surf with the waves arcing under its hull. Scratch and her Red Eye grunts fitted their prisoners with shock collars before marching them up the ramp.

"Where are you taking us?" Brain demanded.

No one answered.

Pete's legs wobbled as he realized they were being taken off the planet. He knew from *SkyWake* that dropships weren't used as attack vessels. Their armour wouldn't last long if they flew into battle against the

Squids' clifftop artillery. The Red Eyes must have other plans for him and his friends.

He took one last look over his shoulder at the battlefield as he climbed up the ship's ramp. He half hoped to see Casey at the bunker about to mount a daring rescue. But he knew that she was already long gone, heading for an adventure beneath the planet's surface. In the distance, at the base of the cliffs, the mind-controlled gamers were digging in, getting ready to launch their assault. He wondered if they would try and scale the cliff face, although he wasn't sure how they'd do that. Before he could work it out, the loading ramp closed, and he was sealed inside the dark interior of the Arcturian vessel.

"Feels like old times, right?" Xander said with a thin smile, tugging at the shock shackle around his neck as they were ushered through the belly of the dropship. Pete smiled, pleased at the camaraderie between them, even though the uncertainty over what Xander was planning made his palms sweat.

The Red Eyes marched the prisoners through the ship and pushed them into seats beside an observation window. There was a shallow vibration as the dropship took off and flew up through the planet's atmosphere and into space. Out of the window, Pete saw an inky canvas dotted with twinkling points of light stretching in all directions.

His mind raced, overwhelmed by the enormity of being so far from home. He half expected to feel his body start to float, weightless. Yet whatever tech the Red Eyes were using gave the ship its own gravity, and his limbs remained as heavy and tired as they'd felt back on Hosin.

Brain and Elite slumped in their seats, staring at the celestial vista in stunned silence. The fight seemed to have gone out of them.

"You know," Xander said, turning to Pete, "part of me feels responsible for all this."

"Getting captured?"

"No! I mean us all being here in outer space. I was the guy who made *SkyWake* famous, right? My channel had over a million subscribers. I just didn't realize I was working for aliens the whole time."

"It's not your fault. No one knew what *SkyWake* really was."

Xander paused. "Do you know the key to being a successful YouTuber?" he eventually asked. "It's your brand. If I say 'Burger King', what do you think of? Whoppers, lettuce, tomatoes and those golden crowns."

Thinking about Burger King made Pete feel hungry. He reached into his pocket, remembering he had a few toffees stashed in there. He felt the cellophane wrappers crinkle under his touch and considered offering Xander one. But it didn't seem the right moment. The YouTuber was on a roll.

"Now, when someone says 'Xander Kane'," the teenager continued, "what do you think of? Annoying show-off with an ego the size of a planet... But you also think: Winner, winner, chicken dinner. Amirite?"

Pete hesitated.

"It's OK, kid. I'm not offended. That's me, that's my brand. Half my followers want to be me. The other half want to punch me. It's my secret sauce." He pushed his fringe out of his eyes.

"I don't really understand," Pete mumbled, flattered to have been picked to be the audience for this conversation but struggling to keep up.

"What I'm saying is this. If I want to stay on brand, I've gotta win. I've got to go back to Earth with my head held high, not like some loser who was abducted by aliens. But to win, I need your help."

"Me?"

"We've been in the trenches together, kid. I need you to be the Luigi to my Mario. The Cortana to my

Master Chief. If we work together, we can go back to Earth and be famous. But first, we've got to stop Casey running around like a loose cannon. We've got to help the Red Eyes rein her in."

"I'm not sure about that," Pete said, suddenly wary. "I mean, she is my sister…"

"And you love her, right?"

"Yeah, I guess." Pete blushed.

"Of course you love her! She's family. That's why you need to stop her. It's for her own good. If your sister carries on like this, she's gonna get herself killed. You don't want that, do you?"

Pete suddenly felt sick. The thought of losing Casey as well was too much to bear. He shook his head.

"Well, we're the only ones who can stop her."

"What can we do?"

"First, we get Casey to surrender. You're the key to that."

"I can't just give her up to the bad guys." Pete pulled a face.

Xander ignored his concerns. "Second, we need to find out what the Red Eyes really want. I don't believe they care about that rock of a planet down there. In *SkyWake* they were looking for some kind of device that the Squids had. If we can work out what they want, maybe we can help them and get back home to Earth. If we pull it off, we'll be heroes."

"Heroes?"

"You bet! Imagine the welcome party they'd throw for us! Everyone would want to interview us. They'd probably even make a movie about our story."

Pete thought about the posthumous medals his dad had been awarded. People had called him a hero too. Maybe helping Xander was the right thing to do.

"We'll all get home?" Pete asked, checking he understood. "Even Casey? We can't leave without Casey."

Xander nodded. "Of course."

"Then count me in," Pete said, relieved by his new friend's confidence.

The YouTuber flashed a smile that showed all of his teeth.

11

I'M SORRY, CAN YOU SPELL YOUR NAME, PLEASE?

When Casey woke, she found herself lying on a four-poster bed in what appeared to be a medieval castle. A cooling breeze brushed over her face, causing silky drapes to flutter at the far end of the room. Beyond them a balcony looked out onto a cobalt-blue sky. A solitary cloud hung in the middle of it, wispy as cotton wool.

She jerked into a sitting position, her head racing. Where on earth was she? She instinctively reached for her plasma rifle before realizing her exo-suit and weapons were gone. She was wearing her jeans and hoodie like she had been before all this started. How much time had passed? She wasn't sure. All she knew was that for the first time since leaving for the *SkyWake* tournament, she felt rested.

She climbed off the bed, struggling to understand her surroundings. After the humid alien beach, the room felt reassuringly familiar. Yet being here made no sense at all. She pinched her arm hard in case she was dreaming. *Ouch!* Obviously not. The drapes billowed in the breeze as if inviting her to step through them.

She felt a sudden rush of vertigo as she walked out to the balcony. She was standing on the top of a tall, slender spire that was buttressed to the side of a castle. Far below her a patchwork of rolling green fields spread out towards the horizon, intersected by a river that meandered across the landscape in a slovenly curl. A volcanic mountain glowed orange in the distance, ringed by an impenetrable forest of gnarled trees. The whole scene looked like something out of a fairy tale.

How could the tunnels under the beach have led here? It made no sense. The sound of footsteps took her back inside, hoping to see her friends. But instead a young woman stood in the middle of the bedroom. She had almond-shaped eyes and pointy elfin ears, and wore a flowing blue dress. Her golden hair was tied in braids and a tiara fitted with a single blue gemstone rested on her head. Casey felt like she had seen her somewhere before, although she couldn't say where.

"Greetings, child," the woman said in a soft, sing-song voice that seemed to appear inside Casey's head without the woman's lips moving. "My name is Xolotl. I am here to represent the Bactu."

"But you're human!" Casey's eyes fell on the woman's pointy ears. Perhaps she wasn't quite human – but she certainly wasn't a Squid.

"I took this form to put you at ease. Someone you would recognize."

"Princess Zelda!" Casey said, suddenly realizing. She knew she'd seen her somewhere before.

"Did we make a mistake?" Xolotl asked, sensing her surprise. "We found her image in your memories. We thought she was someone you admired; someone you would feel comfortable speaking to."

"I always wanted to play as Zelda instead of Link," Casey murmured, remembering the hours she'd spent with her dad and Pete questing through the kingdom of Hyrule in all the different *Legend of Zelda* games. "I loved it when she disguised herself as Sheik in *Ocarina of Time* and convinced everyone she was a boy."

As Casey spoke, Xolotl transformed in front of her. The princess with elfin ears and cotton-wrapped braids vanished and was replaced by a ninja, her face obscured by white bandages.

"Better?" Xolotl-Sheik asked, karate-chopping the air. "Or perhaps you would prefer *this*?"

Xolotl shape-shifted again and turned into a futuristic soldier in an orange battle suit. The soldier pulled off her helmet to reveal a slender woman beneath. She tossed out her hair.

"Samus!" Casey gasped, recognizing the heroine from the *Metroid* games.

It was as if someone had reached into her mind and ransacked it, pulling out familiar odds and ends and laying them in front of her.

"Would you prefer something else?" Xolotl-Samus asked, sensing Casey's distress. The room vanished and Casey found herself in a dimly lit video arcade, surrounded by flashing coin-op machines. She recognized the place. It was FunZone, the video arcade her father had taken her to the summer before he died. A tall figure stood in front of a *Space Invaders* cabinet, his back to her. Casey felt the hairs on the back of her neck stand up.

"Dad?"

He turned round, the light from the screen illuminating his face, and smiled at her.

"No!" Casey shouted, fighting back tears. "This isn't real. None of this is real. Get out of my head!"

The arcade disintegrated around her, peeling away to reveal the castle bedroom behind it. Then that vanished too, and Casey found herself in a featureless white room. The avatar of her dad slowly changed into a Bactu. Casey realized it was Xolotl, now in her true form. Compared with the aliens she had seen in SkyWake, Xolotl looked elderly, perhaps even ill.

We didn't mean to distress you. The words materialized silently in Casey's mind.

"Where are my friends? Cheeze and Fish and the lieutenant?"

They are safe. You have our word.

"It was you who spoke to me on the beach, wasn't it? What do you want from me?"

We need your help, Casey. But first we need you to understand.

Casey felt Xolotl reach deeper into her mind. The room receded and she saw a series of images play out. It was like a movie being projected onto the inside of her skull. She wasn't just watching it. She was part of it.

"What are you doing to me?" Casey gasped.

We're going to tell you a story.

Casey's mind jerked and she found herself racing through space. Below her was a dusty-looking planet shrouded with thick clouds. In a flash, like a jump cut in a movie, she was on its surface, watching Xolotl descend the ramp of a compact spaceship. The alien slithered down the ramp into a barren, prehistoric desert. Imposing mountains lined the horizon, hemmed in by charcoal clouds.

Millennia ago, the Bactu were the galaxy's caretakers. Our role was to search the galaxy for intelligent life and help it evolve.

Xolotl set up a device in the sand. It was mounted on a tripod and stretched up into the air like a mobile phone mast. She touched the mast with a tentacle and a silent telepathic signal was beamed across the planet to its inhabitants.

We didn't dictate or interfere, we simply nudged those that showed promise in the right direction. We helped thousands of species, nurturing and encouraging them to take the next step in their evolutionary journey before leaving them to choose their own path.

As Xolotl's spaceship departed, Casey watched a group of reptilian humanoids emerge from the caves beneath the mountains. They were Arcturians. One approached the device and reached out a cautious hand, as if drawn to it by some invisible attraction. As he touched it, his eyes glinted with new knowledge.

Most species we helped never even knew of our existence. Or, if they did, we became part of the stories they told themselves. They painted pictures of us on cave walls; they built temples to honour us. We were treated like distant, absent gods. But one species set out to find us. The Arcturians, those you call the Red Eyes, were fast learners. They were keen and hungry for knowledge and quick to implement it. We thought, naively, that they might one day become our heirs.

In the blink of an eye, thousands of years whizzed past. Casey watched the Red Eyes' society grow and expand out of the caves. Farmers tilled the barren soil until it began to flourish. Villages sprung up. Then towns, cities, mega-cities and spaceports. Over generations, the Red Eyes transformed their barren, primitive planet into a sprawling hub for interstellar travel.

Arcturian society proved rigid and hierarchical. It prized order above all else. We thought they would use the knowledge we gave them wisely. But they did not. They were obsessed with violence.

Casey watched as two Red Eyes fought to the death on a floating platform that hung above a vast chasm. She recognized the arena from one of *SkyWake*'s cutscenes. It was a Crucible, a place where Arcturians trained for battle and fought one another to gain honour and glory.

Their only aim was to accrue power for themselves.

The scene changed and vast armies of Red Eye soldiers marched in rigid formation across a spaceport launch pad. Standing on a platform, high above the soldiers, stood an emperor in flowing crimson robes. Behind him hung Arcturian flags emblazoned with a clenched, gloved fist. He addressed the crowd, igniting their passion with a warlike speech.

As they ventured into space, the Arcturians conquered planet after planet. Whole worlds fell to them. They killed or enslaved anyone who wasn't like them.

Casey watched as epic space battles blazed across the skies. Red Eye dropships launched troops onto one planet after another. Arcturian overseers and grunts rounded up alien species, hatred burning in their eyes as they put shock collars around their necks. Some were forced to fight in the Crucible to entertain the masses, others were sent to work in chain gangs.

"What were they looking for?" she asked.

Us, the Bactu. They explored every corner of the galaxy trying to find us, remembering our visit from millennia before. Perhaps they thought they could only truly be great once they had fought us. We met them as equals and tried to show them the error of their ways. But the Red Eyes were envious of our telepathic abilities and quickly grew to hate us. Had they come to us in peace, we would have shared our final gift of knowledge with them: how to unlock the power of their minds. But instead, they thirsted for war.

The scene shifted again, and Casey was back on the beach on Hosin, watching wave after wave of Red Eye troops hot-drop onto the purple sand and invade the Squids' home world.

Once, they had worshipped us as gods. Now they believed they had to destroy us to prove themselves. We were forced to defend ourselves, even though we hate violence.

In the tunnels beneath the beach, the Squids fought back with their psi abilities. Whole squads of Red Eyes were brought to their knees as the Squids reached into their minds, making them see things that weren't there and turning them against one another.

In frustration, the Arcturians tried to replicate our telepathic powers using technology. Then, finally, they learned how to create soldiers we couldn't stop.

Casey saw the teen gamers from Earth being fitted with mind-control devices and she finally realized why they'd been abducted. The Squids couldn't repel these mind-controlled human soldiers using their telepathic powers. She saw squad after squad of blank-faced gamers fighting on the beach. This was what was happening on Hosin right now.

"But what do the Arcturians want?" Casey asked quietly, appalled by the brutality of the Red Eyes' quest for domination. "Why are they doing this?"

They want to rule the universe. If they succeed, they will not be benevolent rulers. They will not nurture the weak or encourage the slow. They will be demanding, angry dictators, interested only in remaking everything in their own image.

Casey saw a map of the galaxy expanding before her. Planet after planet fell to the Red Eyes. The last planet was one she recognized. It was her home … Earth.

"You have to stop them!" she cried, terrified at the implications of Xolotl's words. "You said you were caretakers."

We are an old race, Casey. Our time is coming to an end. We wanted to bequeath our power to a species that had the potential to take our place. Long ago, we thought that would be the Arcturians. But we were wrong. They are intent on finding an ancient Bactu device. They won't stop until they have it in their possession.

"The psionic array," Casey said, remembering *SkyWake*'s lore.

The array acts like an amplifier, Xolotl continued, *letting us extend our psi abilities between galaxies and contact other caretaker races. Placed in the wrong hands, though, it could be a super-weapon. The Arcturians think they can use it to dominate the galaxy, controlling other races' minds remotely.*

"Where is this device?"

Hidden far away; and yet closer than you might think.

"That sounds like a riddle."

If it is, it's one the Arcturians have yet to unravel. They are convinced the array is hidden here, beneath Hosin's surface. That's why they're invading and, thanks to their new human army, there's nothing we can do to stop them. Your mind-controlled friends are resistant to our psi powers, and even if they weren't, we don't want to hurt them. Our quarrel is with the Red Eyes, not humans. So, as you see, we need your help.

"What can I do?" asked Casey.

Humans have a hidden gift, Casey. One that's not unlike our psi abilities. That is why you were able to hear us on the beach.

Casey remembered standing in the Rhino's turret, aiming the rail gun at the Phantoms and experiencing that intense feeling of focus right before the Squids reached out to her.

"Flow?" she said, guessing the connection.

What you call "flow" is really just the untapped potential of the human mind. We want to show you how to focus it and unlock humanity's true power.

"You want *me* to do that?" Casey felt overwhelmed. It was too much. She didn't want to be a hero. She just wanted to go home. She shook her head firmly. "I need to find my brother. He's still on the beach somewhere."

Xolotl's tentacles fell still. *Your brother and the boys who were with him are no longer on Hosin. The Red Eyes have taken them prisoner.*

Casey's chest tightened in panic. "No!"

We're sorry, Casey.

"I should never have listened to you! I left Pete behind to go into the tunnels because of you."

If you hadn't, you would have been captured too. Or perhaps worse.

"Where is he?" Casey demanded. "Where have they taken him?"

He's on the Arcturians' command station orbiting Hosin. Even though it made no sound, Xolotl's voice seemed to have become softer inside Casey's head.

"I have to go there," she said firmly. The Squid's calm stillness suddenly made her want to scream.

We need to train you first. We need to show you how to

harness this power you call flow. It is the only way humans can stop the Red Eyes.

"How long will that take?"

Days. Weeks. Months. It is a process that cannot be rushed. But if you stay with us, we can teach you everything we know in time.

"What, like Mind Control and Telekinesis?" Casey scoffed, thinking back to the Squids' psi powers in *SkyWake*.

Xolotl's tentacles rippled, displeased. *We know how much you love your brother, Casey. But you must think of the greater good. If we do not stop the Red Eyes, they will destroy everything you care about. Stay and let us train you.*

"I can't leave Pete alone with the Red Eyes," Casey said. "I just can't. Who knows what they could do to him? Plus there's the other gamers too. I have to get back on the beach. I have to find a way to free them all."

Xolotl stared back at her with rheumy, ancient eyes. The Squid looked resigned, like she had known all along what Casey's answer would be. *You are making a mistake.* There was no anger in Xolotl's words, just weariness. *We brought you here because we believe humans have potential. Perhaps even more potential than the Arcturians.*

Xolotl reached out a tentacle and touched Casey's face gently. She felt a rush of energy. Her thoughts raced like a movie on fast forward, a dizzying torrent of images and feelings.

The tentacle receded. Casey's skin tingled and her mind buzzed.

"What did you just do?"

I unlocked a door. We'll see how far you can push it open on your own.

Before Casey could ask what that meant, another Squid appeared behind her. He was larger than Xolotl and seemed younger, too. One tentacle was shorter than the others, its stumpy end covered in a mass of scar tissue as if it had been severed in an accident or perhaps a fight. Casey realized it was the Squid from the beach.

This is Eldreth, Xolotl's silent voice said. *He will take you to your friends.*

Casey nodded hello. The Squid's head bobbed in reply. When Casey looked back, Xolotl had vanished. Which was freaky, given that the white-walled room had no door.

12

MADE FOR SHARING

The orbital command station was the size of a small moon and shaped like a spinning top. It hung in the blackness of space, gently rotating as it orbited Hosin. Ships flew in and out of it like bees from a hive, a constant stream of traffic going to and from the planet below.

The Arcturian dropship made its approach smoothly, its navigation systems carefully controlling every movement as it entered the space station's belly and came in to land. The docking bay was enormous, the size of several football pitches, and lined with rows of attack craft and dropships. Ground crew and drones scurried between the vehicles, refuelling and repairing them before they headed back to join the battle below.

As Pete was escorted down the dropship's ramp with Xander, Brain and Elite, he marvelled at the sheer scale of the space station. He had seen it in *SkyWake* a million times before, but in reality it was infinitely more impressive.

Looking out of the docking bay into deep space, he could see Hosin beneath them, the two suns breaking over the rim of the planet. His head swam.

How could he be here, so far from home?

At least on Hosin he had been able to feel the purple sand under his feet. But on the space station, deep in outer space, he felt small and lost. He scanned the thousands of stars that hung in the airless vacuum beyond the docking bay and wondered which pinprick of light was Earth. It was impossible to tell.

The Red Eyes forced the prisoners to stand in line as an overseer approached. With his dark grey cloak and cowl, the supervisor looked like a medieval monk. He kept his hood up and his face hidden, issuing orders in a low whisper while gesturing with his hands.

Scratch clamped her fist over her heart in the standard Arcturian salute and bowed respectfully. She spoke in the Arcturians' strange, impenetrable language for a moment. Then, after the overseer had passed, she returned to her squad.

"Are you going to hurt us?" Elite blurted out anxiously, unable to help himself.

"You will be our guests until your Cay See comes to rescue you," Scratch said, letting the translator do its job.

"She won't come," Brain said firmly. "She's too smart for that."

"Cay See comes always for little brother," the alien rasped in halting English, chucking Pete under the chin with her gloved hand. He recoiled from her touch. "I have just learned that the emperor himself is going to oversee our final victory on Hosin," she continued. "We will show him what we do to humans who defy us." She motioned for two of her Red Eye grunts to lead the prisoners away.

The journey took them down into the belly of the space station through corridors bustling with crew and drones going about their business. Each level seemed darker and more imposing than the last. Eventually a door slid open, and they found themselves inside what appeared to be a prison block. A row of holding cells stretched in front of them. Instead of doors, the cells were guarded by energy fields that shimmered and crackled menacingly.

The Red Eyes removed the boys' exo-suits and, finally, their shock shackles, and shoved them all into a cell together. Pete was the last one in. As he stumbled over the threshold, he heard the energy barrier reactivate behind him, sealing all four boys inside. The Red Eye troops vanished back along the corridor without another word.

Brain turned to Xander with a glare. "Great plan, love your work," he sniped.

"Not so long ago we had five plasma rifles pointing at us ready to pull the trigger," Xander said, rubbing his neck where the shackle had been. "We're alive. And if you're alive, you're winning."

Pete looked around the large cell. The walls were bare apart from several stacks of triple bunk beds, and in the wall at the far end there was a sealed hatch that looked like it might be used to supply them with food. His stomach grumbled at the thought. He remembered the sweets in his pocket and pulled one out. They were the golden Toffee Pennies from a Quality Street tin, leftovers from his mum's birthday the week before. He'd swiped them before he'd left the house that morning to eat at the tournament and had forgotten all about them in the chaos until now.

He headed towards the far end of the cell while the others argued, hoping he might be able to snaffle a sweet without anyone noticing. He pulled up short. An orange LED flashed on and off from somewhere in the gloom at the back in the cell. What was it? Pete took a step forward, intrigued.

"Made for sharing," a man's voice whispered in the darkness. He sounded croaky and hoarse, but slightly amused.

Pete jumped in surprise. "Who's there?"

"Made for sharing," came the voice again.

Pete squinted into the shadows. He could just see the outline of a man sitting on one of the bunks at the very back of the cell. Before he could say anything, a hand reached out towards him, palm up. The hand gestured to Pete, as if asking him for a sweet.

Pete hesitated, letting his eyes adjust to the darkness. He could see a man, lean and tall and dressed in a simple grey jumpsuit with Arcturian symbols on the chest, sitting on the edge of a bunkbed. A metal device looped from his temples around the back of his skull. The orange LED flashed on its side. It looked like he was wearing a set of headphones that had slipped backwards off his head.

The prisoner stood up and took a step forward, emerging from the shadows. He wore dog tags on a chain around his neck. Pete's hand instinctively reached for his dad's dog tags that Casey had given him. Was this man a soldier too?

"Made for sharing," the man repeated.

Pete, unnerved, yelped and dropped the sweet on the floor. As he darted back to his friends, he heard the rustle of a plastic wrapper being unfurled. It was followed by a low sucking sound.

"Mmmm," murmured the voice in the darkness. "Toffee Pennies. My favourite."

13

I'M NOT IMMATURE, YOU'RE IMMATURE!

Casey followed Eldreth as he slithered through a series of blank, white corridors, his tentacles writhing beneath his body. She had so many thoughts rattling around inside her head she didn't really know where to start. First there was the news that her brother had been captured; then the Squids' crazy belief that she could help them find some super-weapon. Finally, the realization that these creatures were apparently friendly after all. They weren't the monsters *SkyWake* had made them into.

Not "apparently". We are *friendly.*

The voice in her head had a sarcastic tone. If it was possible for telepathic words to have a tone.

Casey stopped in her tracks. "Did you say something?" She was fed up of these aliens barging into her mind without so much as a polite knock. The Squid's response was impossible to read. He was strange and mysterious, like one of those creatures that swim in the darkest depths of the ocean.

How rude. Bactu do not swim.

"Please get out of my head!"

My name is Eldreth. I am two thousand years old, and it is my job to act as your escort. I can be silent if you prefer. But it is more entertaining this way.

"Not for me," Casey said. She looked around the white-walled corridor. "Why are we walking? Why don't you just jump us to wherever we're going? None of this exists, does it?"

You're correct. This is simply a psychic construct.

"Where are we really?"

Imagine billions of Bactu, lying in the dark caves beneath the surface of Hosin, each connected to the others by its tentacles. That is how we live. We use our psychic powers to create this. Eldreth waved a tentacle around the corridor. *It's a shared space where our minds meet. We call it the Mindscape.*

"Doesn't it get chaotic?"

We are more disciplined than you humans. We know how to put aside our egos and work together for the greater good.

Casey bristled. "That's unfair!"

Is it? Humans have a reputation for being wild and unruly and … immature. The Squid's head bobbed, amused.

"You know, for someone who's thousands of years old, you're really rude."

I've seen enough of humanity to know that you're not as advanced as you think you are. I mean, you haven't even mastered space flight yet.

"We've been to the moon!" Casey said, feeling like she had to stick up for the human race.

Oooh! You managed to fly to a barren lump of rock right on your doorstep. That's like a baby being proud of itself for learning how to pass wind.

"We're more advanced than you think," Casey said crossly.

Tell that to your friends.

Casey blinked and suddenly found herself in an enormous room that looked like a penthouse suite in some kind of Las Vegas hotel. A huge window looked out across an urban sprawl, neon signs from the casinos below flashing in the night sky.

She gasped, not at the view, but at the chaos inside the room. Six small monkeys raced around, swinging from the light fittings and screeching in wild abandon. A long banquet table, which had been laid out with platters of food, had been overturned in a mess of melted ice cream, chicken nuggets and barbecue sauce. A Bluetooth speaker pumped out an upbeat K-pop song, the Korean lyrics occasionally punctuated by a nonsense English phrase. In the far corner of the room, a fluffy, knock-kneed ostrich with thick eyelashes was trapped on a bouncy castle. It flapped its wings helplessly with each new bounce, unable to escape its inflatable rainbow prison.

Fish and Cheeze stood in the middle of the chaos, laughing hysterically. They were dressed in their normal clothes, all their weapons and armour gone. Casey realized with a jolt that Cheeze was standing even though he wasn't wearing Scratch's power suit.

"Casey! You're here too! Come see this, it's nuts! We can get anything we think of!" Fish clicked his fingers and a gleaming Harley-Davidson motorbike appeared. He jumped in the saddle and tried to kickstart it. Nothing happened.

"You forgot to imagine any petrol," Cheeze scoffed. "Try this."

He closed his eyes, concentrating, and a skate-boarding deck appeared. He jumped on it and skated across the room before pulling off an impressive ollie kickflip. "Oh man, it feels so good to do that again."

Dreyfus stood outside on the penthouse's balcony, bathed in the city's neon glow. He rolled his eyes at Casey, unimpressed by the boys' antics.

What was it you were saying about being mature? Eldreth asked.

Casey sighed and pushed up the sleeves of her hoodie. "Boys!" she shouted, trying to get their attention over the noise of the monkeys and the K-pop beat. "BOYS!"

Everything in the room stopped at the same time, and the music faded away. Even the ostrich managed to stop bouncing. It hopped unsteadily from one foot to the other on the undulating plastic castle and blinked its thick eyelashes at her expectantly.

Fish and Cheeze hung their heads like naughty school kids.

"Sorry, Casey," Cheeze mumbled. "We just got carried away. I mean, none of this is real. I realized that the moment I found myself walking. It happens sometimes when I'm dreaming." He stamped his feet on the suite's carpeted floor. "Then Fish said he was hungry, and a burger appeared out of nowhere and we discovered that anything we thought about would appear, and…"

"Things got a bit out of control," Fish chimed in, reddening. "It's like when you spawn eggs in creative mode on *Minecraft* to build, I dunno, a zombie zoo or something."

"Ooh, zombies!" Cheeze said. "Why didn't we think of that sooner?"

"We could play paintball with them!" Fish closed his eyes, ready to summon some living-dead corpses.

"Don't you dare!" Casey warned him.

A sarcastic voice filled all their heads. *What a pity. I would have loved to have seen zombie paintball. Millions of years of Bactu evolution and we never thought to use the mindscape for anything so sophisticated.* Eldreth raised his tentacles above his head, as if cheering on his favourite football team. *Go, humans!*

"Please get rid of all of this," Casey said firmly, pointing to the mess. Eldreth shrugged and everything that the boys had imagined disappeared into thin air.

It took Casey a good twenty minutes to update Cheeze and Fish on everything Xolotl had told her. The boys kept on interrupting, wanting more details about Xolotl's ability to shift between video-game characters and asking what it was like to see Zelda and Samus in real life. Casey indulged them before circling back to the key points.

First: the Red Eyes had captured Pete and the others and taken them to the space station orbiting above Hosin. Second: the Squids were on the verge of defeat. They couldn't stop the mind-controlled gamers by using their telepathic powers and, even if they could, it was not their way to use force – they didn't want to hurt them. Once Hosin was overrun, the Red Eyes would realize that the array wasn't here. Then what would they do to the Squids? Torture them? Enslave them? It didn't bear thinking about.

"So, what you're saying," said Dreyfus, who had listened to Casey's explanation from the balcony with a grave expression, "is that we're not just here to save the gamers. We have to save the Squids as well?"

Yes, Eldreth agreed, *I find that hard to believe too.*

"What can we do?" Cheeze asked. "There's just us. We don't have an army. We don't even have a full squad. We've lost our medic and our sniper."

"We're stuffed," Fish agreed. "We'd need a miracle to stop the Red Eyes."

Casey remembered what Xolotl had said about flow and untapped potential. She wasn't sure how to tell the boys about it. It sounded crazy.

Cheeze rubbed his chin, deep in thought. "You said the Red Eyes took Pete and the others to an orbital command station, right?" he asked. "Just like the one in the game?"

Casey nodded.

"Well," he continued, "that must be where they're broadcasting the signal from – the one that's controlling the gamers."

"Can we block it?" Casey asked.

"It's too powerful for that," Cheeze said. "But if we got up there, we could try to deactivate it."

"What is this orbital thingamajig, exactly?" asked Dreyfus, who knew nothing about *SkyWake*.

"In the game, the Red Eyes use it as a staging post for invading planets," she explained. "I guess you'd call it a military base in space."

"Like the Death Star," Fish chipped in helpfully.

Dreyfus arched his eyebrows. "And you want us to just waltz on in there without an invitation?"

Casey shrugged. "I'm open to better suggestions."

"How will we even get to it?" Fish asked. "We don't have a spaceship or anything."

Eldreth's voice entered all their heads at once.

That is where I come in.

"You?" Casey asked, surprised.

Yes, I will be your taxi driver to the stars.

14

ENTER: THE GAME DESIGNER

The prisoner sat on a bunk sucking his toffee coin. Pete watched him cautiously. He seemed shy and a little wary of the new arrivals. He kept his eyes on the floor, refusing to acknowledge their presence. It had clearly been a long time since he'd had any human contact.

"What's your name?" Pete asked, timidly. The rest of the boys hung back and watched. Pete swallowed and tried again. "I'm Pete. These are my friends: Xander, Brain and Elite."

"Pete," the prisoner repeated, shyly making eye contact. "Pete. Pac-Man. Pac-Man. Pete." He pointed to himself.

"This guy's cracked," Xander muttered. "What's he going on about old video games for?" The teenager stalked over to the energy field that sealed them inside the cell. It buzzed threateningly, mirroring his own annoyance.

"Maybe 'Pac-Man' is a nickname?" Brain suggested.

"How long have you been here?" Pete continued, offering the prisoner another toffee. The man eyed it hungrily without taking it. He continued slurping on the one already in his mouth.

"Suck them slowly, that's the trick," he said haltingly. "Don't rush. Make them last."

"I don't know if this dude will be able help us," Elite murmured.

"Question is, how did he get here?" Brain asked, cocking his head on one side. "I don't think he was in the shopping centre with us. He looks like he's been here a while." His eyes took in the prisoner's Arcturian jumpsuit.

Pete didn't like the way everyone was talking about this man as if he couldn't hear them. "Why did you mention *Pac-Man*?" he asked. "Is it because you like video games?"

The man stopped sucking and looked at him properly for the first time. The intensity of his gaze made Pete flinch.

"I *love* video games," he said, leaning forward. "Do you?"

"Y-yeah," Pete stammered.

The man's eyed widened eagerly. "Which ones?"

"All video games, really," Pete replied. "I used to play *Space Invaders* with my dad. He had a proper coin-op arcade machine."

The prisoner chuckled, growing in confidence. "*Space Invaders*? That's older than both of us put together. Tell me about some new games. What have I missed?"

"How long have you been here?" Pete asked.

The prisoner gestured towards the wall, where a series of marks could be seen scratched into the metal. There were a lot of them. "Years," he said. "I made a scratch for every meal they gave me. Three scratches a day. You can count them if you like." He chuckled mirthlessly as he waved towards the thicket of scratches.

Pete stared at the man, wondering what he'd been through here on his own. He couldn't even begin to comprehend it. The prisoner changed the subject before he could ask him more.

"Tell me, what games are popular now?"

Pete looked at the others, uncertainly. They motioned him to go on. "Lots of people like *Fortnite*," he said after a pause. "It's a battle royale."

"A battle royale?" the prisoner repeated.

"You parachute onto an island, and you have to kill everyone else to win. Lots of people play it. Plus, *Overwatch*, *Call of Duty* and *Rocket League*. That last one's like football, but with cars instead of players. My favourite game, though, is *SkyWake*…"

The effect of these words on the prisoner was instant. He spat out his toffee and leaped off the bunk. "*SkyWake?*" he cried, getting up in Pete's face. "You've *played* it?"

Pete retreated, scared.

"Tell me!" the prisoner shouted. "I need to know!"

"Bruv!" Elite said, pushing him away from Pete. "Back off!"

The man collapsed onto his bunk and held his head in his hands. "What have I done?"

"You know about *SkyWake*?" Brain asked.

"Of course I do," the prisoner sighed. "I designed it."

The boys looked at one another in surprise.

"You made it for the Arcturians?" Pete asked incredulously. "But they're using it to turn gamers into soldiers!"

"I didn't want to design it," the prisoner said, picking at the implant in his head in despair. "They fitted me with this thing and forced me to. You have to believe me. I didn't want to do it."

"Great," said Xander from the other side of the room. "He's not just a nutter; he's the nutter who got us into this mess. Give him another toffee. He's earned it."

Later that night, after the hatch in the wall had delivered trays of tasteless brown paste for them to eat, Pete sat down beside the prisoner on his bunk at the back of the cell. The man hadn't said a word since their earlier conversation, lost in his own thoughts, and the others had given up on getting anything useful from him. Exhausted from their ordeal, the boys had crashed out on the bunks and quickly fallen asleep. Pete, though, couldn't rest without knowing more. He felt sorry for the prisoner and was intrigued to know his story.

"When I was a kid, I always loved video games," the man told him. "Platformers, shoot 'em ups, first-person shooters. You name it, I played it. I wanted to go to college and study games design. But my dad kicked me out when I was sixteen and I joined the army instead. I was so proud to wear that uniform. 'Private Simon Ross, reporting for duty, SIR!' They say when you join the army, you get somewhere to call home. I didn't have a home, so it seemed like a good deal. Looking back on it now, though, I'm not so sure."

Pete took the two remaining toffees from his pocket and offered them to the soldier. Private Ross only took one. "You have the other one," he smiled. "Made for sharing, right?" He seemed to be getting used to having company again, his rusty social skills slowly coming back to life after years on his own on this alien command station.

"And then you got abducted and ended up here?" Pete asked.

"They killed everyone in my squad." Private Ross nodded, his eyes moistening. "I was the only survivor."

"But why you?" Pete asked. The minute he said it, he realized the question sounded ruder than he'd intended.

"I've asked myself that so many times," Private Ross said, taking no offence. "I think they just wanted someone to interrogate. At first they were keen to know about our military capability on Earth. But then they started asking me questions about our culture, our entertainment. I tried not to give them anything useful. I thought talking about video games would be a safe topic. I mean, I could talk about gaming all day long. I expected to bore them senseless. But they found a way to use what I was telling them for their own ends." He paused, pensive. "What is *SkyWake* like to play?" he asked.

"Oh, it's amazing," Pete whispered in hushed reverence. "The most immersive shooter ever."

"Is it popular?"

"You bet! People all over the world play it. You'd have made a great games designer."

Private Ross looked quietly pleased by this.

"I used everything I'd learned about games design to build it. How to balance teams. How to structure a good map. The Red Eyes used their supercomputers to put it all together, but they couldn't have done it without my ideas." He paused and sucked his toffee. "Your friend Xander is right, you know. It *is* all my fault."

"No," Pete said. "That's not true. They forced you to do this." He eyed the device that wrapped around the back of his head. Its orange LED flashed rhythmically.

"This was one of the first mind-control devices the Red Eyes made," the prisoner explained, letting his fingers run over it. "As soon as they put it on me, I wanted to build the game for them. It gave me no choice. But you know the worst thing? I enjoyed it. I enjoyed using everything I'd taught myself about video games to build something new and unique. That's why I feel so guilty."

"But they're not controlling you any more?" Pete asked, eyeing the device suspiciously.

"They don't bother with me any more, not since I delivered *SkyWake* for them. They just keep me around for the fun of it, I think. Anyway, this is old tech now," he added, tapping the device in his head. "Their new mind-control devices are much more powerful. As soon as they put them on you, you're nothing more than a mindless zombie."

Pete felt sorry for him. The guy had been snatched from Earth and dragged halfway across the galaxy as a prisoner of the Arcturians. He thought back to when he'd been separated from the others, in that maze of corridors in the off-limits section of the shopping centre. He guessed they both knew what it was like to be alone and afraid.

They sat in silence a moment.

"What do the Red Eyes actually want?" Pete asked. "Abducting soldiers. Building video games. Turning gamers into zombies. Seems like a lot of trouble to go to just to destroy the Squids."

"They don't care about the Squids," Private Ross told him. "What they're really looking for is an ancient device they think they can use as the ultimate weapon."

"I remember!" Pete said, recalling *SkyWake*'s opening cinematic. "The intro talks about it whenever you load up the game. My sister always skips that bit, but I liked to let it play. You're talking about the psionic array, right? Hidden by the Squids?"

The prisoner nodded. "The Arcturians are obsessed with it. When I was making *SkyWake*, it was all they kept talking about. They showed me all the info they had on it." He stopped and glanced at the surveillance cameras on the ceiling.

"Can I trust you, Pete?" he said, dropping his voice low.

"Of course you can."

Private Ross paused again, as if trying to decide whether or not to say more. In the gloom all Pete could see was the faint glow from the LED as it flashed.

"The Red Eyes aren't going to find the array."

"But they've almost overrun Hosin," Pete said glumly. "It's over."

"It doesn't matter. They're looking in the wrong place. The array isn't on Hosin."

Pete felt his throat constrict. He knew something bad was coming. "Where is it then?"

Private Ross glanced at the surveillance camera again. He dropped his voice until it was barely audible at all. "Have you ever heard of the Chariots of the Gods?"

Pete shook his head.

"Some people say that aliens came to Earth thousands of years ago, back when we humans were still grubbing around in the mud. Can you imagine? You're standing there in your loincloth trying to make fire by rubbing two sticks together and a great big UFO suddenly appears in the sky in a blaze of light…"

"You think the Squids came to Earth?"

"Maybe," the prisoner said, unwrapping his last toffee and popping it in his mouth. "There was a theory that aliens helped humans build structures like the pyramids in Egypt and South America and those big stone heads on Easter Island. I don't know if it's true or not. But when the Red Eyes forced me to create SkyWake, they uploaded all their data about the Squids into my head. I saw a symbol I recognized…"

"Where?"

Private Ross glanced at the camera. "I've probably said too much already. All these years with no one to talk to and now I'm gabbling away. It's too risky."

"Hold on," Pete said, determined not to lose the chance to find out what was really going on. He darted over to where Elite was sleeping and gently eased the rapper's notebook and pencil from his hand. "Here. Write it down."

"I can do better than that. I can draw it."

The prisoner took the pencil and, shielding the pad from the surveillance camera, he started sketching. Pete watched as he drew two vertical rectangles next to one another. They looked like lumps of rock. Pete stared. What if he didn't have a clue where it was? He didn't want to seem stupid. But, as the image began to take shape, he realized he'd seen it somewhere before. The prisoner drew another rectangle horizontally across the two vertical ones. It looked like a doorway. Then he drew a huge circle like the sun rising above it.

Pete gasped. "I know it! It's St—"

Private Ross quickly clamped a hand over Pete's mouth. "You mustn't tell anyone!" he hissed sharply. "The Red Eyes don't know what that symbol means. They don't even know it's important and they definitely don't know it's on Earth." This last word was barely audible.

Pete sat in silence staring at the sketch of two standing stones with a third laid across them. It was a picture of Stonehenge, the best-known prehistoric monument in England. Pete remembered a school trip to see it. The visitor information centre had even had a little display board that made fun of a crazy theory that the monument was built by aliens. Turned out it maybe wasn't so crazy after all.

"You're saying the Red Eyes have been searching the galaxy for the array and it's been with us all along?" he whispered in excitement.

"If you were the Squids, where would you hide something like that?" Private Ross asked. "On your home world? Or in a distant corner of the galaxy where no one would ever think to look?"

Pete could see the logic in that. But one thing still bothered him.

"In the game, it said the Squids buried parts of the array in different locations," he said quietly. "So, where are the other pieces?"

"The Chariots of the Gods, right?" The prisoner smiled, tickled by the genius of it. "All those ancient sites on Earth are the perfect locations to hide things. Temples in the jungle, ancient cities on the sides of mountains, crumbling monuments in deserts. I think they scattered the pieces all over. But the last part, the key to it all, is here." He tapped the picture in the notebook. "Once you get this, you can activate the whole array."

With that he ripped out the page, rolled it into a paper pellet and surreptitiously popped it in his mouth. "Not as good as a toffee. But we'd better not take any chances, right?" He swallowed hard and smacked his lips. The camera didn't notice a thing.

"So, what do we do?" Pete asked. "How do we stop them?"

Private Ross swung his legs over the side of the bunk despondently. "I don't think we can."

"You mean we're gonna be prisoners for ever?" Pete lay back on his bunk and stared at the ceiling. He sucked the nub of toffee that he still had in his mouth, his mind racing. He couldn't stay here. He knew that for certain. He had to get home.

He was so distracted that he didn't notice Xander. The YouTuber was sitting across from him on his own bunk on the other side of the shadowy cell. He hadn't seen the prisoner's sketch, but he had overheard enough of the conversation to make his eyes glint greedily in the gloom.

15

TAXI DRIVER TO THE STARS

Casey had only a vague memory of being carried through the Squids' underground nest alongside her friends. She had an image of thousands of writhing Bactu bodies covering the floor and walls and ceiling. The creatures lay in a huge jumble, attached to one another by their tentacles while their minds roamed in the shared space that they created together using their telepathic powers.

She wondered what it must be like to live like that. Then it occurred to her that she maybe already knew. Was it that different from playing an online game, inhabiting a shared virtual world with others? She thought about how often she had dreamed about *SkyWake*'s maps. The online spaces she shared with her teammates could sometimes feel more real and intense than the physical world of home and school.

Maybe that was what it was like for the Squids, too. Their shared world was like a game world, a place to play and connect with others.

She had no recollection of being taken on board the Arcturian shuttle. When she next blinked her eyes open, she found herself strapped into one of the padded crew seats, Dreyfus, Cheeze and Fish beside her. Eldreth was already busy at the ship's controls, his tentacles slithering over the buttons as he powered up the engines. He was too big for the Red Eye ship, his bulbous head dwarfing the instrument panels.

"We're on a spaceship?" Casey asked, her voice dry in her throat. She wondered how long it had been since she last spoke out loud, rather than in her head.

"It's Arcturian," Cheeze noted. "A Ranger class shuttle. The Red Eye fleet use them for reconnaissance. What's it doing on Hosin?"

Eldreth spoke to them all at the same time, his voice appearing inside their minds. *We captured it in the Red Eyes' last attack. Xolotl thought it might come in useful one day.* The Squid's tone, as always, sounded slightly mocking.

"How do we get onto the space station?" Casey asked and, before the words were off her lips, she knew the answer. The details just appeared in her head. "Oh, you're going to pretend to negotiate with the Red Eyes."

"I wish you'd stop info-dumping straight into our minds," Dreyfus grumbled, looking at Eldreth. "It's very disconcerting."

It's very efficient, Eldreth said, prepping the ship for launch. *You humans waste so much time talking around things instead of getting straight to the point. Even now, after everything you've all been through, there's so much you haven't told one another. You're supposed to be friends, but you find it impossible to communicate. You don't even know each other's real names.*

"We talk all the time," Fish said. "It's what humans are good at. We never stop talking."

The problem is, you talk without saying anything.

"That's harsh…"

But true. Eldreth turned to Cheeze and eyed the boy's battered Red Eye power suit. *Take Cheeze, here. He's never told you how he ended up in a wheelchair and he's trying not to complain about wearing this Arcturian power suit, even though it's hurting him. He wishes he was back in his wheelchair, but he's worried about letting you down by making a fuss.*

"It was a stupid skateboarding accident," Cheeze mumbled. "I was trying to grind down the handrail on the library steps. And yes, this suit hurts to wear, but I'll be OK."

Casey felt a pang of guilt for not asking him how he was doing. She'd just assumed he was coping.

And you, Eldreth continued, looking at Fish. *You're glad you and Casey are friends, but you still have an issue trusting girls because of what happened with your mum. You miss her, even though you're still angry with her for running off with that double-glazing salesman.*

"You can't tell everyone that!" Fish cried, blushing. "It's, like, private."

And you, Lieutenant…

Dreyfus leaped out of his seat, wagging his finger in warning. "Try that on me you overgrown cephalopod, and I will chop you up into calamari."

Eldreth's tentacles rippled mockingly. *I know how much you regret the choices you've made in your past. The impossible choices about who lived and who died. They weigh heavily. That's why this fight against the Red Eyes is more than just another mission for you. It's personal, isn't it?*

Dreyfus sat back down. He stared at the display screens on the bridge, his face set like concrete. Casey realized why he was always so grumpy. He wasn't angry at them; he was angry at himself.

There was a judder as the shuttle's engines powered up, lifting them upwards through a dark, craggy chute that led from the Squid caves out onto the clifftops on the surface of Hosin. The shuttle's afterburners roared as it ascended into the sky. Casey stared at the monitors as they left Hosin behind and watched the battlefield on the beach becoming smaller and smaller. She saw Eldreth watching it too.

"It must be awful to see your planet being attacked. If Earth was invaded like this, I'd want to be down there fighting with them."

Now it's your turn to read my mind, the Squid replied. *You're right. The future of Hosin hangs in the balance. I just hope Xolotl's faith in you humans isn't misplaced.*

Casey swallowed hard. "We're going to stop this."

The Squid turned to face her. *Do you know what your problem is, Casey? You still think it's possible to win without losing anything. Sometimes sacrifice is the price of victory.*

"Just tell me what I need to sacrifice, and I'll do it," she said.

You probably won't know what it is until the time comes.

Eldreth swiped the nav computer with a tentacle, throwing the shuttle into a tight arc as it burst through the planet's upper atmosphere. The teammates were pushed back in their padded seats as it accelerated.

It wasn't long before the space station appeared ahead of them, glinting in the light from the solar system's two suns like an enormous tiara. It was huge and majestic, a celestial vision. For a moment, Casey almost forgot that it was full of Red Eyes intent on intergalactic domination.

They stared at it in awed silence until a grumbling sound echoed around the shuttle, ruining the moment. Fish crossed his arms over his belly, trying to silence it.

"Dude," said Cheeze. "Seriously?"

"I can't help it! I haven't had a proper meal since we left Earth. That imaginary food back on Hosin didn't fill me up at all."

"Maybe the Red Eyes will have some food for you," Casey suggested.

"What do the Red Eyes even eat?" Fish asked, curious. Eating was always his favourite topic of conversation. "They never mention food in the game."

They like to eat the bones of their enemies after they crush them in battle, Eldreth said. *Sometimes they even drink the blood of the fallen using their helmets as cups.*

Fish's face fell. "For real?"

No. I'm just messing with you.

"Not cool, Eldreth. Not cool at all."

An alarm rang out across the bridge.

"Someone's hailing us," Cheeze said, recognizing the sound from *SkyWake*.

Everyone keep quiet and stay off camera, the Squid ordered as he opened the comms channel. A Red Eye overseer appeared on the monitor, his face hidden beneath his cloak's hood.

"Regleth hef?" the overseer croaked as he saw Eldreth. Arcturians always sounded angry, Casey realized. It was such a harsh language. She couldn't ever imagine one Arcturian telling another that they loved them. Every word they spoke sounded like a declaration of war.

"What's he saying?" Fish whispered to the others. Without a translation device, they couldn't understand anything.

Eldreth replied to the overseer in Arcturian. It was, Casey realized, the first time she had heard a Squid speak out loud. The sound was strange, almost bird-like. After a brief exchange, the overseer pulled the hood back from his robes in a victorious flourish and Casey saw the creature's reptilian head beneath. His forked tongue darted out and licked his lips as if in anticipation of a meal. Then the comms screen went dead, and the shuttle jolted sideways.

"What's going on?" Dreyfus demanded.

They've locked onto us with their tractor beam. I no longer have control.

"What did you say to them?" Casey asked.

I told them I was an emissary from Hosin coming to negotiate the planet's surrender.

"No wonder he looked so excited," Dreyfus grunted. "He thinks he's about to go down in the Arcturian history books."

We should move quickly, Eldreth said. *We need to be ready.*

"Somebody tell me we have a plan," Fish said, looking at them all. "We do have one, don't we?"

16

FEELING TILTED

The infiltrator suit was strange and uncomfortable to wear. It was made of a silver, stretchy material like Lycra that clung tight to Casey's skin as she pulled it on. In *SkyWake,* infiltrators were designed to be stealth ninjas, creeping behind enemy lines and hacking the enemy's systems using their special cloaking suits. In real life, Casey felt like she was wearing a Halloween costume. The suit covered her hands and feet and even her head and face, with tech fitted into the hood that augmented her sight and patched her into the shuttle's comms system.

"Run me through the plan one more time," Fish said. "I can't get my head around it."

"C'mon, Fish," Cheeze complained. "We've been through it ten times already."

"You can never check the plan too many times,"

Dreyfus interrupted. "In the army we call it 'The Six "P"s'. Proper Planning and Preparation Prevents Poor Performance."

"Right," Cheeze said with a weary sigh. "It's like a magic trick. You get people to watch one hand while the other hand does all the sneaky stuff." He spun his hands in the air to make his point.

"Just imagine I'm an idiot," Fish said. "Walk me through it slowly."

Cheeze rolled his eyes. "You *are* an idiot."

I could just reach into your brain and implant the information, Eldreth offered. *It might save us an hour or two.*

Fish recoiled from his outstretched tentacle. "No way! I hate it when you do that. I never know what you're going to dig up in there."

Are you thinking of that time you kept telling elderly people to be careful not to die—

"No one needs to know about that," Fish snapped. He looked at the others, embarrassed. "I was four, OK?"

"Listen," Casey said, elbowing Cheeze to stop him from smirking. "As soon as the shuttle lands, Eldreth will give himself up to the Red Eyes."

I'll tell them I'm on a diplomatic mission to negotiate Hosin's surrender and I'm bringing two prisoners as a gesture of goodwill.

The Squid pointed at Dreyfus and Fish with two of his tentacles. Dreyfus didn't look particularly happy about it, but he didn't interrupt.

"That's the hey-look-over-here! part of the trick," Cheeze explained to Fish. "The rest is the sneaky-behind-everyone's-back part. While Eldreth delivers Fish and the lieutenant as prisoners, Casey will stealth her way across the space station. I'm going to hide on the shuttle and give her instructions over the comms on how to turn off the control signal. When it's offline, we can free all the gamers and—"

Kick some serious Red Eye butt.

Everyone stopped and stared at Eldreth in surprise. The young Squid shrugged defensively and pointed an accusatory tentacle at Fish.

I was just saying what he was thinking.

"Please stay out of my mind," Fish muttered.

As the shuttle arrived in the docking bay of the space station, Casey watched Cheeze prep the comms system. He grimaced as he sat in front of it, his power suit jerking as if it wasn't fully in his control.

"How are you holding up?" she asked, sitting in the seat next to him.

"All good."

She could tell he was lying. The suit was clearly

causing him pain. It was designed for Red Eyes, not humans.

"Eldreth says there's a bunch of Red Eye gear in the hold," she told him. "Maybe you could find some new power armour. It might work better."

Cheeze finished prepping the comms and looked down at the suit that had previously belonged to Casey's nemesis. It was bulky and heavy, its jet-black contours harsh and unwelcoming. It didn't "suit" him at all, she thought.

"I just want my wheelchair back," he confessed. "You know, it's funny. Before I got hurt, I was always on wheels. I spent every minute skateboarding. Popping ollies was my life. Then, after my accident, I ended up on wheels in my chair. It became an extension of me. I customized the frame and everything just like my old skateboarding deck."

Casey remembered his lime-green wheelchair stuffed with wires and all kinds of hacker gear. She could see why he'd miss it. It wasn't just a mobility aid. It was part of his identity.

"As soon as we get home, we're going to get you a new chair," she promised. The words sounded hollow, even to her ears.

Cheeze's face was pale and serious. "You

really think we can make it back to Earth?"

Casey tugged at the infiltrator suit. She wasn't looking forward to pulling the hood over her face – she already felt suffocated by the tight material as it clung to her body. "I don't know," she admitted, her voice despairing. "All I've done so far is make bad decisions. Brain and Elite went with Xander. Even Pete left me."

"None of that was your fault."

"Wasn't it? I must have done something to make Pete leave. I mean, he chose Xander over me. Xander!"

"Forget about that guy. He's a tool. You're better than him. That's why the Squids reached out to you."

"Xolotl said humans are more powerful than we realize," Casey told him, remembering her conversation with the alien. "She wanted me to stay on Hosin and train with her. She thinks 'flow' is the key to unlocking the secret power of our minds."

"What, like, telekinesis and stuff?"

"Yeah," Casey said. It sounded silly saying it out loud. "She thinks human brains have untapped potential, something we need to use if we're going to take the next evolutionary step."

"It sounds like levelling-up in a video game. Why didn't you stay?"

"I couldn't leave Pete," Casey told him, trying not

to shout in frustration. "He's out there all alone. He needs me." She took a deep breath. It felt like a great weight was pushing down on her. She didn't want to be in charge. She just wanted to go home.

Fish came over to where they were sitting. He had obviously been listening to their conversation. "You know what your problem is, Casey?" he said, putting his hands on his hips like he was immensely proud of the insight he was about to reveal.

"Do tell us," Cheeze replied, annoyed by the interruption.

"You're tilted. It's like in a match when everything's going wrong and you're just not feeling it. You make one mistake and then another and, before you know it, you're smashing your controller to pieces in anger. Being tilted is hard to come back from. It gets into your head, messes you up. You can't aim. You can't shoot. You can't win. You need to reset."

"What can I do to fix it?" Casey asked.

"Wellllll…" The boy puffed out his cheeks. "When I get tilted, I usually just rage-quit and go and eat the scraps out of the deep fat fryer in my dad's chip shop."

"Nice one, loser," Cheeze muttered, giving him a playful shove.

Casey thought about it. Maybe there was some

truth in what Fish said. Maybe being tilted was the opposite of going with the flow. Maybe she did need to stop and reset. But how could she? Pete and the others had been captured; Hosin was almost overrun; and she had a mission to carry out. All she could do was push on.

The shuttle jerked, ending the conversation. The tractor beam had pulled them into the docking bay. Through the shuttle's viewing windows Casey could see two squads of Red Eye grunts waiting on the landing pad.

We need to be ready, Eldreth told them.

Casey activated her infiltrator suit, pressing the touchscreen that sat under a flap of material on her right sleeve. There was a hum as the suit powered up, its adaptive surface refracting the light around her. She stared at her hands as they slowly faded away in front of her eyes. She was turning invisible.

Across the shuttle bridge, Dreyfus and Fish looked on in awe.

"Tell Pete I'm coming."

"I will," Fish nodded, serious for once.

And then, just like that, she completely vanished.

It only took the Red Eyes a few minutes to secure the shuttle's crew. Eldreth opened the hatch and slithered down into the loading bay, leaving a trail of sticky residue on the shuttle's ramp. He had two tentacles wrapped around Dreyfus and Fish as if they were his prisoners.

While the Red Eyes were distracted by the new arrivals, Casey snuck into the docking bay, moving slowly to ensure she stayed invisible. She crouched beside the loading ramp as a squad of Red Eyes marched into the shuttle to search it, their boots just inches from her cloaked face. Cheeze was somewhere inside, hiding. She prayed he wouldn't be discovered.

As Eldreth spoke to the overseer in Arcturian, Scratch and her squad stepped forward to take the human prisoners into custody. She hissed at Dreyfus, recognizing him from the shopping centre. She still hadn't forgiven him for cutting her out of her power armour.

"I thought you were dead," her translator said, rendering the words in English.

"You'll wish I was before this is over," Dreyfus threatened, defiant as ever. He didn't flinch as a shock shackle was placed around his neck.

Scratch turned to Fish.

"Cay See?" she demanded in halting English. "Where is she?" The alien's eyes darted towards the shuttle's ramp, blinking sideways in that strange reptilian manner. For a terrible moment, Casey thought she'd been spotted.

Fish quivered as Scratch drew closer, petrified of her scaly skin and sharp teeth. He began to sweat, uncertain what to say.

"She's not here," he stuttered.

Scratch hissed and her tongue flicked angrily between her lips. Behind the prisoners, the Red Eye squad returned from searching the shuttle. They marched back down the ramp and sealed the hatch shut. The overseer, content the shuttle was empty, barked instructions to Scratch. The alien clamped her fist to her chest and signalled her troops to escort the prisoners across the loading bay.

Casey, invisible in her suit, watched them go. She suddenly felt very alone.

"Cheeze?" she whispered into her throat mic.

Silence.

She waited a minute or two, the panic rising in her chest.

"Are you there?"

He still didn't answer.

She stepped forward, feeling weirdly disembodied by the fact that she couldn't see her feet or arms. At the edge of her vision, a meter fitted into the suit's eyepieces charted how much light disturbance was happening when she moved. The brighter the room, the more visible her movements would be. She watched it spike with each step she took, the meter moving from green to yellow to red. When she stopped, the gauge settled back down to a safe steady green. She would need to move slowly and cautiously to remain invisible.

She crept into the centre of the docking bay, watching as the Red Eye ground crews prepped the attack ships waiting to go down to Hosin. At any moment, she expected to be discovered. It was so strange to be hiding in plain sight like this.

"Cheeze?"

No answer.

Where was he? She couldn't do this without him.

A drone flew by, oblivious to her presence. She felt the heat from its power core as it sailed past. She jumped in surprise and the light meter on her suit spiked from the green into the yellow. She froze, afraid that someone might have seen the disturbance in the air.

"I'm here," Cheeze said over the comms. "They turned the shuttle upside down, but they didn't even come close to finding me." Casey tried not to shout with joy. "It took me a while to get the systems back online after they shut everything down," he continued. "Are you all right?"

"I'm freaking out," she confessed. "I feel totally exposed out here. They're going to see me."

"They won't. Trust the suit. Trust me. I'm gonna be your eyes and ears. I've got you." She heard him punching buttons. "Where are you?" he asked. "I'm looking at the docking bay feed, but I can't see you at all. Give me a wave or something."

Laughing, Casey blew a kiss in the direction of the shuttle. The light meter on her display barely left the green zone.

"See anything?"

"You're a total ghost," Cheeze said. Then, sensing the amusement in her voice, he added, "What did you just do?"

"Nothing. I'm just glad you're here. Now, tell me how to get to the signal controlling the gamers so I can shut it down for good."

17

HIDE AND SNEAK

Infiltrators had never been a big part of *SkyWake*. The Squids' telepathic powers made the Red Eye stealth suits next to useless. Lots of players had complained that the Squids' powers were too "OP", or overpowered, and called for them to be "nerfed" by the game's developers. Eventually the class fell out of favour as Red Eye teams simply refused to add them to their squads.

On the orbital command station, though, the infiltrator suit was invaluable. The Red Eyes would never suspect anyone was creeping around wearing one. As she moved across the docking bay, Casey tried to remember everything she knew about playing stealth games. Unlike shooters, stealth games were action puzzles. Instead of rushing in, all guns blazing, the key was to avoid combat. Stealth players went *around* their enemies rather than through them, sneaking past danger.

Casey headed towards the blast doors that led from the docking bay into the rest of the space station. She hugged the wall and moved slowly, keeping an eye on the light meter on her display. The key to staying invisible was to avoid making any sudden movements. *SkyWake* players had even invented a special "crouch walk" to slow them down in the game. She was just thinking about trying it in real life when Cheeze's voice crackled over her headset. He'd hacked into the space station's camera systems from the shuttle so he could guide her.

"Wait up," he advised. "Ground crew coming your way. Stay on the left side of the doors."

Casey crouched low as the doors slid open with a hiss. She hadn't expected this to be so nerve-wracking. Two Red Eye engineers stepped through, pushing a replacement engine thruster for one of the attack ships on a trolley. Unlike the Arcturian grunts, they wore jumpsuits instead of power armour. Casey waited until they had passed and then slipped through the doors before they shut behind them.

The space station itself was much busier than she'd expected. Dozens of Red Eyes were walking along the corridors, saluting one another with a fist clamped over their chests as they went about their business. Drones flew among them, effortlessly correcting course as they avoided the soldiers.

Casey was in the eye of the storm.

She padded softly along the corridor, hugging the wall. Every moment, she expected someone to see her. Being this close to alien soldiers who would happily capture – and maybe even kill – her was terrifying.

"Your heart's thumping," Cheeze said over the comms.

"You can hear it?" Just how loud was it?

"No, doofus. I'm getting a read-out from your suit. I can see your pulse, heart and breathing. They're all spiking."

Casey paused as a Red Eye grunt passed, pressing herself against the wall to avoid him. It was like playing blind man's buff.

"I'm freaking out," she said, keeping her voice low. The suit was fitted with a throat mic that let her talk in a whisper.

"What did the Squids mean when they said humans needed to level up?" Cheeze asked as Casey crept forward again. She knew he was trying to take her mind off things.

"I don't know. They think humans have some untapped potential, something they can nurture. Their whole deal is helping other species, right? They fly around the galaxy trying to help others evolve. They want to do the same for us, I guess."

"Sounds creepy to me. Who put them in charge?" He paused a moment. "Did they tell you what powers they can unlock for us? Is it like in *SkyWake*? All those Squid abilities like Mind Control and Psi-Blast, and what was the other one called? Telekinesis! They could lift a Rhino into the air and just drop it on top of your squad and pancake you. Maybe you'd be able to do that if you stayed and trained with them. Maybe we all could…"

Casey turned the corner into the next corridor. Arcturian symbols were printed at the junctions, indicating different parts of the vessel.

"Hold up. I need to open the next set of doors for you," Cheeze said.

Casey heard him muttering to himself as he worked out how to override the door's locking system. She was glad he was with her. She knew he felt frustrated because he wasn't as mobile as the rest of the team, but they couldn't have got this far without his hacking smarts. Teams were like that. Everyone brought a different skill set. That was what made the Reapers so strong. They complemented one another brilliantly.

She sighed, realizing she still had to get her team back together.

The doors opened and she passed through, then snuck up a stairwell. Three levels up, she found herself on a covered walkway that stretched over the docking bay. Below her she could see the Arcturian dropships and fighter jets being rearmed by the ground crew. As she watched, a new ship arrived. It had sculpted wings, a crimson body and a painted white stripe that ran across its roof from nose to tail. It was fancier than any of the other vessels she'd seen.

Six Red Eye squads waited to greet it, standing in regimented formation with an overseer at the head of each group, their cloaked heads bowed low. The ship's hatch slid open, and a lone figure dressed in flowing crimson robes stepped out.

The emperor! Casey nearly gasped aloud, recognizing him from *SkyWake*. The Arcturians' supreme leader stepped down the ramp, followed by four imposing soldiers carrying high-tech lances. The overseers bowed as the emperor removed his helmet with a flourish. Beneath it lay a reptilian face that was severe and haughty.

Unlike the other Arcturians, the emperor had a circle of folded skin around his neck like an Elizabethan ruff. It reminded Casey of a nature documentary she'd seen about an Australian lizard called a frilled dragon that uses its frill to scare away predators. The emperor didn't look like he had to worry about anyone trying to eat him, but the frill made him hold his chin high, giving him a regal look that suited his status as the leader of the Arcturians.

"What's *he* doing here?" Cheeze asked. Casey looked over at the shuttle and saw her friend's shadow in the cockpit looking out, just a few metres away from the new arrival.

"He must have come to oversee the surrender of Hosin," Casey guessed. "The Red Eyes have been waiting years for this moment."

The emperor walked past the assembled Arcturian soldiers leading a creature on a chain. It looked like a lynx with large yellow eyes, long, fine whiskers and pointed ears. The creature's fur was red with white tiger stripes. It padded past the ranks of alien soldiers on soft paws, its eyes fixed forward as if the troops were beneath its interest.

A delegation of Red Eye overseers approached the emperor. Behind them stood Scratch. The alien seemed eager to convey some news to her leader. Casey stared, fascinated. A drone flew past her on the walkway, bringing her back to her senses. Time was short. She had to get to the control room where the signal enslaving the gamers originated.

She tore herself away from the scene below and continued into the next corridor. It was the same as all the others, apart from a computer terminal set into an alcove in a wall. A holographic Arcturian head floated above the terminal, waiting for instructions. As Casey slid past it, the head spoke a few words in Arcturian, seemingly to itself. She jumped, startled.

"The terminal's fitted with motion detectors," Cheeze explained. "It knows you're there and it's asking if it can help you."

"Well, it could start by not scaring the life out of me," Casey muttered, shooting the head an angry glance. It continued to hang in the air, oblivious.

"Hold up!" Cheeze warned. "Multiple Red Eyes coming your way."

Before Casey could react, the doors at the far end of the corridor slid open. Two squads of Red Eyes quick-marched through them, two abreast and filling the corridor.

"What do I do?" she hissed in panic. If she stayed

where she was, they would crash straight into her. She looked around wildly. There was nowhere to go.

"The alcove!" Cheeze said.

Casey glanced over her shoulder at the floating reptilian hologram. It was silent now, but if she went back towards it, wouldn't it start speaking again?

"It'll give me away!"

"Hold on, I'll try and hack it."

Casey crouched, her eyes fixed on the Red Eyes marching towards her. They moved in lockstep, boots thudding, kit rattling as they charged down the corridor. She guessed their haste was something to do with the emperor's arrival.

"Problem," Cheeze said hurriedly over the comms. "I can't access the terminal." She could hear the rising panic in his voice.

Casey's heart thumped inside the skintight invisible suit. She didn't know what to do. She could run back down the corridor ahead of the Red Eyes, but they'd see her if she moved that fast. She could jump into the alcove and trigger the AI, but they'd hear it talking to her.

Whatever she was going to do, she had to do it quickly. The Red Eyes were almost on top of her. They marched shoulder to shoulder in two perfect lines, a slim gap between each column. Casey stared at the terminal. The floating holographic head flickered expectantly.

"Run!" Cheeze yelled over the comms. "Get out of there!"

"No."

Casey moved into the centre of the corridor. She waited until she could see the very reds of the approaching soldiers' eyes, that deep, malicious crimson that flickered in their helmet eyepieces. At the very last moment, she twisted her body, pivoting on the balls of her feet like a dancer. She turned herself sideways and slipped into the gap between the two columns of soldiers.

They stormed past on either side, so close she could smell the strange metal alloy of their suits. She closed her eyes, waiting for the inevitable impact as they bumped into her.

But it never came.

In a flash, it was over. Still standing in the middle of the corridor, she opened her eyes to see the two columns of Red Eyes continue on their way, oblivious to the fact they had just passed her. She breathed out in relief, her body shaking with adrenaline.

"Sweet baby Jesus!" Cheeze yelled, almost bursting

her eardrum in his excitement. "What just happened?"

"Didn't you see?" she asked, looking up at the surveillance camera on the ceiling.

"You're invisible, you idiot!" laughed Cheeze. "I can't see you at all."

The sound of the Red Eyes' boots receded down the corridor.

"I can't believe it actually worked," Casey began, "I thought—"

She cried out in surprise as something whacked her between the shoulder blades and knocked her off her feet. Her back exploded in pain and she hit the floor hard, the light meter on her suit flashing into the red. Dazed, she looked up to see a drone that had come flying down the corridor behind her spinning out of control. The lump of flying metal had crashed right into her back, unable to sense her invisible presence, and had been knocked off course. It bounced off the wall before crashing to the floor in a shower of sparks.

The marching Red Eyes, alerted by the commotion, spun around just in time to see the flicker of refracted light from Casey's infiltrator suit. They raised their plasma rifles and ran back towards the spot shouting at one another in Arcturian.

"OMG, OMG, OMG!" Cheeze gabbled over the headset.

Casey lay on the floor, stunned. Her suit glitched and flickered, its circuits taken offline by the impact from the drone. As it powered down, the outline of her body slowly appeared, materializing out of thin air. The Red Eyes trained their guns on her.

The acrid taste of defeat burned her mouth like bile. How could she have come this far for it to end like this? She cursed herself for standing in the middle of the corridor, gloating like an idiot, as the Red Eyes passed her. Like a *Fortnite* player who does a victory dance after a firefight and then gets insta-killed by another player who's snuck up behind them.

One of the Red Eyes grabbed Casey and hauled her off the ground, grunting something in Arcturian. The others circled around her, laughing. Casey felt a rush of anger. They were nothing but bullies. Intergalactic bullies who wanted to shove everyone around. She listened to their mockery, digging her fingernails into her palms. The pain cleared her mind as a cold shower clears away sleep.

In a flash, she felt her mind sharpen and her senses heighten. She recognized the sensation. It was like flow, only it was stronger this time. Stronger and purer than anything she'd ever experienced before. She had a sudden image of Xolotl standing in the white-walled room back in the mindscape, telling her about the untapped power that lay deep within the human brain.

I unlocked a door. We'll see how far you can push it open on your own.

A firefighter, a friend of her dad's, had once told her about trying to put out a blaze in a tower block. He said you never opened a closed door in a burning building because the sudden rush of air you created would make the flames in the room behind the door explode like a fireball.

What would she unleash if she opened Xolotl's door?

A Red Eye grabbed her from behind, pinning her arms to her sides. Another started to slot a shock shackle around her neck, fumbling with the mechanism as he tried to clamp it in place. She only had seconds in which to act. The minute it locked around her neck she'd be unable to finish her mission. The gamers would remain the Red Eyes' slaves for ever; Pete and the Reapers would never get off this space station and the Squids would be wiped out.

She clenched her jaw tight. These bullies couldn't win. She wouldn't let them.

She felt a rush of energy moving through her body, lighting up her nervous system like a pinball machine. The power seemed to be coming from somewhere deep inside. She realized it was hers to do whatever she wanted with. She held her hands out in front of her, palms up, and turned towards the Red Eyes as if she were surrendering.

She took a long, deep breath and …

Fffffff-THWUMP!

A psi-blast burst out of her hands and ripped through the corridor in a series of invisible concentric circles as if a stone had been dropped from a great height into a still pond. The force of the blast blew both squads of Red Eyes off their feet. They slammed into the walls and fell to the ground, stunned. Their power suits crackled, the circuits fried.

Casey was the only person left standing, her hair flapping in the breeze.

She looked from the incapacitated soldiers to her empty hands in wonder.

"Oh my God!" Cheeze shouted. "*Casey?* Are you there? All the cameras just went offline. I can't see anything."

"I'm here," Casey said. "I'm OK. At least, I think I am."

"What just happened?" Cheeze asked, his words tumbling over one another. "I saw you raise your hands and then everyone was flying all over the place and the feed cut out... Tell me you didn't just do that!"

"I think I did."

Casey's head felt like it was spinning in a blender. Some huge raw energy had just passed through her. She looked down at the floor and saw a red drop appear in front of her. Then another and another. Each spot blossomed into a little crimson flower. She dabbed a hand to her nose and felt a wet warm stain spreading across the fabric of her infiltrator suit's hood.

"Oh no," she groaned, "I'm bleeding."

18

IT'S TIME TO MAKE A DEAL

Pete was woken by the sound of voices. He'd fallen asleep on his bunk after his conversation with Private Ross and had dozed fitfully, his rest punctuated by indistinct nightmares. He sat up and rubbed his eyes, feeling just as exhausted as when he'd closed them.

Brain stood at the foot of his bunk, examining the energy field that sealed the cell. It crackled, as if sensing the boy's presence. Elite sat near by, quietly rapping to himself with his notebook in hand.

"Hey, brainiac, I'm stuck. I need a rhyme. What rhymes with 'distance'? I've got 'existence' and 'resistance'. What else?"

"Bit busy right now," Brain said impatiently. Elite put his notebook away and came over to see what he was up to.

"What do you reckon it's made from?"

"I'm not sure yet." Brain watched the field like it was a puzzle. "I need to study it some more."

Elite rolled his eyes. "I'm gonna stick my hand in it," he said, impatient as always. "Gotta know what we're dealing with, right."

"Uh, I'm not sure that's a good idea," Pete warned, climbing off his bunk. He admired Elite's enthusiasm, but he couldn't help but think the boy was terminally reckless. In *SkyWake* that could be a useful asset, but in real life not so much.

"Pete's right," Brain said. "No telling what this is."

"I thought you were into science, bruv," Elite complained. "You love *Star Trek* and Dr Spock and all that stuff. This is an experiment."

"*Mr* Spock," Brain corrected him. "Dr Spock was a guy who wrote a bunch of manuals about how to look after babies."

"So, let's do a Mr Spock experiment and see what happens."

"Sticking a wet finger into a socket is not how you experiment with electricity. You need to test a hypothesis in a way that's safe."

"What's the worst that will happen? I'll get a shock? I can take it."

Elite reached out his hand towards the energy

field. It crackled angrily. He paused, uncertain. Pete guessed he was too proud to back off.

"Here," Pete said, taking his house keys from his jeans pocket, "let's try these." He tossed them into the energy field. There was a zap, like an electric fly killer chalking up another victim, and the keys were blasted to atoms.

Elite gulped.

"Good call," Brain said, patting Pete's shoulder. "This idiot would have melted his hand off." He tapped the wall beside the entrance. "I'm guessing there's a power device somewhere inside here. You can tell from the way the field oscillates."

Elite whistled, impressed. "I don't know how you know all this stuff, brainiac. You're like, super smart. At school, I struggle with everything. Maths 'n' English are, like, my Kryptonite. Plus, science and French and, well, everything really… I mean, I can't even find a rhyme for 'existence'. What kind of an emcee can't rhyme proper?"

Brain abandoned his investigation with a sigh. "I can't be that smart. If I was, I would have gone into the tunnels with Casey."

Across the room, Xander cleared his throat. "You guys really are dumbasses," he told them. "The only way we're gonna get out of this mess is by giving the Red Eyes what they want. And, right now, what they want is Casey. We deliver her up to them, we negotiate safe passage back home."

"That's a terrible plan," Brain said, shaking his head. "Especially for Casey."

"If you've got a better one, *Brain*, just let me know," Xander challenged. He glanced at his watch theatrically. "Any time now would be good…"

Brain said nothing. Pete could tell he didn't have an alternative plan, and that it was eating him up inside.

Elite turned to Pete. "You ain't down with this whole giving-Casey-to-the-Red-Eyes plan, are you? She's your sis."

"It's not Pete's fault she lost the plot," Xander snapped. "She made her choices."

"Maybe we can find something else they want," Pete suggested. He glanced quickly over at Private Ross, who was playing on Elite's phone. He'd discovered *Candy Crush* and was busy flicking the screen. He didn't seem to be listening.

The sound of footsteps outside the cell brought the conversation to a sudden stop. The energy barrier crackled and deactivated, then two new prisoners were shoved into the cell by the Red Eyes.

"Fish!" Elite and Brain shouted in unison as they saw their friend, closely followed by Dreyfus. The boys jumped on their teammate in celebration. Fish pushed them off and tugged at his crumpled T-shirt petulantly.

"Hey, watch the threads!" he muttered, then burst into a big grin. "Good to see you guys."

"Where's Casey?" Pete demanded, his eyes darting to Dreyfus.

"And Cheeze?" Brain added.

"They're not with us," Dreyfus said, shaking his head. "We don't know where they are." He didn't say anything more, deciding to be economical with the facts in case the Red Eyes were listening.

Fish looked around the cell in mock disdain. "Not exactly the Ritz, is it?" He noticed the prisoner sitting on the bunk at the back and stared at him suspiciously, taking in the implant sticking out of his skull and his Arcturian jumpsuit. "Who the heck is that?"

Dreyfus followed his gaze and gave a start of recognition.

"*Private Ross?* Is that you?"

The prisoner gasped and then stood to attention – his body rigid, his back straight. He whipped his hand up to his temple in a tight salute.

"SIR!" he barked.

Dreyfus returned the salute, mirroring the rigid pose. The two men stared at each other a moment. Pete looked between them, wondering what was going to happen next. He could see two teary streaks running silently down the prisoner's cheeks.

"At ease," Dreyfus said gently. And then, noticing the implant, he added, "What the hell have they done to you, soldier?"

Private Ross let his hand fall to his side. He stood there unsteadily a moment before his legs buckled beneath him. The lieutenant darted forward, catching his comrade before he fell.

"I've got you," he said.

"I tried to fight them, LT," the prisoner said, his face sallow. "But they got inside my head." Dreyfus put an arm around his shoulders and led him to the nearest bunk. Pete thought there was something almost fatherly about the way the older soldier treated him. "They used me to build the game *SkyWake*," Private Ross continued. "They took everything I knew about video games and used it against us. I'm sorry, sir."

"It's not your fault, son," Dreyfus replied. "I'm sorry we let them take you. That *I* let them take you."

While the soldiers caught up, Pete grabbed Fish.

"What happened to Casey after we got split up?" he demanded. "Is she OK?"

"She's, um…" Fish began and then hesitated, noticing the surveillance cameras staring down at them. "Hey, are those things watching us?"

"Yeah," Brain warned him. "Be careful what you say."

Fish stared at the camera. The camera stared back at him. It was a stand-off.

"Just tell me about my sister," Pete begged. "Did she find the Squids? Is she coming to get me?"

Fish shuffled his feet uneasily.

"Come on," Brain encouraged him. "Spit it out."

"She's not coming," Fish said, making sure the camera was watching. He wanted whoever was on the other end of it to hear this. "Definitely not. No way. Not ever."

Pete's heart froze and his face fell. "Why not?"

"The Squids kept her and Cheeze on Hosin as …" He paused, trying to choose the right word.

"… hostages," said Dreyfus decisively from across the room. "They're holding them hostage. They know the Red Eyes want Casey."

"Yeah," Fish agreed, eagerly. "That's it. Hostages. And they sent us here as …" His words dried up again.

"… prisoners," Dreyfus growled.

"Yeah, bang on," Fish continued. "We're prisoners. The Squids say they're going to surrender. They've come to negotiate with the Red Eyes." He looked at the camera again. It was still staring at him. He hoped whoever was watching had bought his performance.

Pete couldn't believe what he was hearing. "I thought the Squids were going to fight back," he said in a hollow voice. "That's why Casey went to them." He felt as if he'd been punched in the stomach. If the Squids weren't friendly, then Casey really had made the wrong decision, hadn't she?

Xander, who'd spent all this time watching this from his bunk, tutted. "See," he said. "I was right all along." Fish looked like he was about to say something more to Pete, but he clammed up as the surveillance camera's circular lens twisted and whirred, zooming in on him.

Later, Pete listened as the others chatted. Fish was asking Private Ross about *SkyWake*'s design, quizzing him on the game's plasma rifles and the infamous "shake 'n' bake".

"*SkyWakers* always thought it was an exploit, a bug in the code," Fish said.

"No, it was real," the prisoner explained. "The Red

Eyes have been trying to take Hosin for years. But whenever they go into the tunnels under the beach, the Squids defeat them with their psi powers. So, the Arcturians started programming their guns with a self-destruct sequence in case they got captured. They turned them into booby traps. They're vicious like that, the Red Eyes. They think being taken prisoner is a sign of weakness. Their whole culture is about war and violence."

There was a ping and the hatch in the wall opened. Trays of nutritional paste waited for them. Pete felt too depressed to be hungry. He didn't even smile when Fish, permanently ravenous, dipped his finger into the brown paste and stuck it in his mouth.

"It doesn't taste of anything!" the Scottish boy cried, outraged.

"It's a perfect balance of nutrients to keep you healthy," Private Ross explained. "If you close your eyes, you can trick yourself into thinking it's a sirloin steak."

Fish closed his eyes and took another mouthful. He shook his head. "Nope. Not working." He shoved the tray aside with a sigh. "I'd give anything for a burger right now."

Pete sat on the edge of a bunk in the shadows, lost

in his own thoughts. He was still in shock over the news that Casey's plan had failed and that the Squids weren't going to fight back. He felt abandoned. Maybe Xander was right. Maybe they were on their own out here and maybe the Reapers didn't have a clue what they were doing. How could they? They were just kids, after all.

The bunk's mattress sagged slightly as Xander sat down beside him.

"It's rough, buddy," the YouTuber sighed. "I don't know what else to say to you. I'm sure your sister didn't mean for things to turn out like this. But the thing is, if Casey's not coming, then the Red Eyes don't need us any more."

Pete rubbed the back of his neck. It felt rigid with tension. "What will they do to us?"

"I dunno," Xander said, puffing out his cheeks. "Probably just throw us out of an airlock or something." He waited to let that sink in before adding, "If only we had something else we could give them."

He looked at Pete expectantly.

"Like what?" Pete asked. He couldn't shake the feeling that Xander was a step ahead of him.

"I heard that nutter talking to you last night," Xander said, dropping his voice into a conspiratorial whisper. "The Red Eyes are looking for the psionic array, right?" Pete nodded cautiously. "And who knows where that is?"

"He does," Pete said, looking round at Private Ross, who was talking with Dreyfus.

"Not just him," Xander corrected Pete, flicking his fringe out of his eyes, "but *you*, too. Don't you?"

Pete swallowed hard and tried not to give himself away. How much had Xander heard?

The YouTuber stared at him intently.

"I'm not supposed to talk about it," Pete muttered, staring at the floor.

"That's good, kid," Xander said, his voice smooth as velvet. "You need to keep that secret safe. It's your ticket out of here."

"How do you mean?"

"If you can convince the Red Eyes that you know where the array is, they'll give you whatever you want."

"How do I do that?"

Xander cracked his knuckles and smiled a winning smile. "Do you know the best thing I learned from being a streamer?"

"How to make videos?"

"No! How to make *deals*. I've put together all kinds

of deals. Advertising, product endorsements, you name it. I'm like the Donald Trump of streamers. I don't even bother with an agent. I do all my own negotiating with the platforms, ad companies and developers."

"I don't understand."

"What I'm saying is, let's use what we know and negotiate a deal. If Casey's not coming, you're gonna have to rescue yourself. Let me be your agent and we'll broker the best deal anyone this side of the galaxy has ever seen. Agreed?"

Pete felt like there wasn't a choice. Without Casey he really was on his own. Maybe throwing his lot in with Xander was all that was left. "Deal," he said.

With that Xander jumped to his feet and stood directly under the surveillance camera. He waved at it like he was trying to send an SOS.

"Hey!" he shouted. "Me and the kid need to talk to you. We know where the array is. Send someone quick. And don't keep us waiting."

Pete gulped. He hadn't expected things to move this fast.

"What's going on?" Brain demanded.

"I'm getting you losers out of here," Xander replied, jabbing his finger in Brain's chest.

Before anyone could say anything more, the energy

field deactivated and two Red Eye grunts appeared in the cell's doorway.

"Well, that was quick," Xander remarked, impressed. "Guess you really want to know."

The grunts gestured to him to step forward. The teenager grabbed Pete's wrist and pulled him after him.

"He knows where the array is," Xander told the aliens. "I'm his representation. You want to broker a deal, you go through me."

"Pete!" Private Ross shouted, standing to his feet and knocking a tray of food paste onto the floor in the process. "What are you doing?"

"He's doing what you should have done years ago, you toffee-sucking loser," Xander snapped. "He's saving himself."

With that, Xander dragged Pete into the corridor beyond the cell. The energy field crackled back into place behind them. Pete looked over his shoulder to see the boys and Dreyfus looking after them in bewilderment, not quite sure what had happened. Private Ross's face was filled with horror.

"Pac-Man—" Pete called, desperate to try and explain himself to his new friend, but the barrier's orange glow was impenetrable.

19

KILL THE SIGNAL

"We need to talk about what just happened," Cheeze's voice said in Casey's ear as she moved into the communications centre.

"Not now," she told him, stepping into the shadowy room. The lights were dimmed, which was just as well since her infiltrator suit was no longer completely invisible. When she'd powered it back on, the red patch from her nosebleed could still be seen. Casey had caught sight of her reflection and seen a splodge of blood floating in mid-air. It wasn't exactly stealthy.

"But what did you do back there?" Cheeze pressed her. "You threw those Red Eyes across the room without laying a finger on them. It was incredible."

"Not now," Casey repeated, firmer than before.

"At least tell me you're all right. Your vital signs are

going off the scale. Your heartbeat looks like you just ran a minute mile."

"I'm fine," she snapped, although she had to admit she didn't feel fine at all. She had no idea how she'd saved herself from the Red Eyes. It felt like she'd tapped into something deep in the back of her mind, a power that she never even knew she had. It scared her.

The communications centre was a honeycomb of walkways, each higher than the next. She followed the waypoint that Cheeze had uploaded to her suit and climbed out onto a narrow gantry. A jumble of cables ran along it and disappeared into an electrical control panel halfway down the gantry. It looked like some kind of junction box.

"Are you sure we're in the right place?" she said into her throat mic. "I was expecting something a bit more sophisticated."

"The main control room is heaving with Red Eyes," Cheeze explained. "But this is the relay for the signal that's being beamed down to Hosin. If we can cut the connection here, it'll give the gamers a chance to free themselves from the mind-control devices."

Casey stared at the panel. She had no idea how to operate it. "Just tell me what to do."

Silence.

"Cheeze? Are you there?"

No reply.

Casey waited, hoping it was just a problem with the comms. The seconds turned into minutes. The only sound was a faint hum from the power cables that ran along the wall.

"Cheeze? What's happening?"

A burst of static startled her.

"Casey!" Cheeze said, his voice hoarse with panic. "We're too late."

"But I'm at the control panel," Casey said. "Just tell me what to do."

"No, you don't get it. The Red Eyes have stopped the advance on Hosin. I'm patched into their battle net. All the channels are lighting up with new orders."

"You mean they've captured the planet?" Casey asked, her heart sinking. She thought of Xolotl and the Squids, powerless in their underground tunnels as the mind-controlled gamers stormed inside. If the Squids couldn't repel the gamers with their psi powers, it would be a bloodbath.

"No, they haven't taken Hosin. They've ordered a retreat. They're pulling everyone back to the space station."

"Why on earth would they do that?" Her mind

flashed to Eldreth, Fish and Dreyfus. Did it have something to do with them? Had the plan to find the others gone wrong?

"I don't know!" Cheeze said. "But I'm in the Red Eyes' battlenet and they've issued a final retreat order to everyone on the planet. The gamers are being loaded back onto the dropships."

"Can't you override the command?"

"They've taken the signal offline. The overseers on the beach are issuing the orders now. We're too late to do anything from here."

Casey sagged against the wall, drained. How could she have come this far for nothing? If they couldn't free the gamers, there was no way they could get back home. Even if she managed to be reunited with Pete and the others, they'd just be back where they started. They were stuck here, light years from Earth on an enemy alien space station. Xolotl was right. She'd failed at the first hurdle.

"There must be something else we can do," she said into the comms.

"Get back to the shuttle," Cheeze said. "We need to talk to the Squids and come up with a new plan. I'm uploading a route to your map. If we can get a message to Hosin, maybe they can tell us what to do."

"But what about Fish and the lieutenant and the others? And my brother! Are we just going to leave them here?"

"I don't know what else to do. I'm sorry…"

Casey inched back along the gantry, leaving the control panel behind. Her mind raced with questions. Why would the Red Eyes cut the attack short? What would Xolotl say if Casey returned to Hosin without Eldreth? How would Pete react if he knew she had been here and left without him? It was all so complicated. So many choices to make, so many variables, so many consequences … and none of them good.

Cheeze was silent. She guessed he was asking himself the same questions.

She hurried down a corridor towards the docking bay. She was looking forward to getting back to the shuttle and out of this suit. Being invisible wasn't half as much fun as she'd imagined.

"Casey, stop!" Cheeze said suddenly. "Don't move."

She froze as, at the other end of the corridor, the blast doors opened. The emperor entered, accompanied by his imperial guard and overseers, and leading his lynx-like pet on its lead. He was walking quickly, clearly eager to get somewhere, and jabbering in Arcturian to his entourage. Whatever he was saying, it was obvious that something major was going down.

Casey pushed herself against the wall and closed her eyes, hoping no one would see the blood from her nosebleed floating in front of her. She just had to stay still for a moment and not—

Something pressed against her leg.

Something cold and damp and … *inquisitive*.

Casey's muscles tightened in panic. She opened her eyes a crack, already guessing what had happened. The lynx had stopped beside her and was sniffing her thigh. It might not be able to see her, but it could definitely smell her. A low growl gargled in its throat.

The emperor, oblivious, tugged on the beast's lead and barked a harsh instruction at it. But the animal didn't move. Its hackles rose on its back, the fur sticking upright in a ridge as if charged with static. The creature stared right at where Casey was standing. Its whiskers twitched and it bared its yellow teeth as it growled. Its breath smelled like fried meat and garlic.

Everyone turned to look at it.

Casey didn't wait to see what would happen. She rolled past the animal and between the legs of the confused overseers. The emperor pulled on the beast's lead, trying to control it as it snapped at the air. Back on her feet, Casey sprinted towards the doors.

The Arcturians couldn't help but see the flash of movement and the strange red splodge that floated in the air. The lynx roared, furious at the deception and yanked so hard on the emperor's chain that it slipped free. The creature tore blindly after Casey as she raced along the corridor. The imperial guard, convinced that this was an assassination attempt on the emperor, gave chase.

"Run and hide" was the infiltrator protocol on being discovered. The aim was to put enough distance between yourself and whoever was after you, then stop and blend back into your surroundings. But, with the beast on her tail, Casey didn't dare follow protocol. She knew it would sniff her out in a heartbeat. Even if it didn't, the blood seeping into her suit would definitely give her away.

Casey ran down the stairwell and into the corridor beyond, charging blindly forward. Her suit's light meter flashed red, and alarms buzzed in her ears, horrified at the speed at which she was moving. She ignored them and broke into a sprint, feeling relief at being able to move freely at last, now that her infiltrator cover was blown.

"This is bad! This is so bad!" Cheeze muttered as she ran.

"I need directions!" Casey yelled, willing him to focus.

An alarm began to pulse through the corridors. So much for stealth; the whole station knew she was here now.

"They're locking everything down," Cheeze said, panicking.

"Give me directions! I'm running blind!"

"Yes… Directions! Hold on," Cheeze muttered, coming back to his senses. She could hear him typing, pulling up schematics of the space station. "Head left!" he shouted.

Casey took a sharp turn. The lynx was closing in on her, its lithe body pounding along the corridor, its nose following her scent. Its chain clattered behind it like an unruly tail.

"There's a drone hub right ahead," Cheeze told her. "Try and lose them in there."

"That thing will smell me wherever I am!"

"There's no other option!"

Casey hurtled into the drone hub. It was a dark storage room where the machines repaired and recharged themselves. Inactive drones were stacked in shelves in the gloom, their sleek metal chassis glinting in the low-level lights. There were hundreds of them.

"I'm gonna try and hack them," Cheeze said. "Maybe I can create a distraction."

"Hurry," Casey said, seeing the silhouette of the lynx appear in the doorway. It sniffed the air then slinked inside, moving cautiously as if expecting to be ambushed at any moment. Casey crawled into a corner, trapped.

There was a hum from the rack of drones as six or seven of them powered up. Their lights came on one by one.

"I'm booting them up," Cheeze told her. "Be ready to run when I tell you."

Casey pushed herself against the wall as the lynx moved towards her. She tried to focus. Maybe she could blast the lynx across the room, she thought, just like she had with the Red Eyes. But the power didn't seem to come. It was too hard to concentrate with the creature sniffing her out.

Maybe Xolotl was right. Maybe she did need to learn how to use these powers.

The lynx padded towards her, its pink, wet nose twitching as it sniffed the air.

"Almost there," Cheeze said on the comms.

Three Red Eyes stepped inside the drone hub. Two of them were the emperor's robed imperial guards, carrying their lances at the ready. The other was

Scratch. The alien sealed the door behind her as she entered.

"We know you're in here, girl," Scratch said, her forked tongue darting between her lips as she voiced the words in Arcturian and waited for her translator to render them in English.

Casey froze and the lynx, smelling her fear in the air, snarled. Scratch grabbed its lead to keep it under control and signalled the emperor's guards to fan out. Their burning red eyes seemed to narrow as they watched for the slightest sign of movement in the gloom.

Casey looked at the shelves of inactive drones. The boot-up sequence was taking too long.

"I'm coming, Casey," Cheeze said. "Just need another minute…"

Before Cheeze could say anything more, Casey disconnected the comms. She didn't want the Red Eyes to know she had a helper. Then she lifted the flap on her forearm to reveal the suit's controls and tapped the touchscreen.

The suit flickered and glitched as it powered down and Casey materialized in front of the approaching Red Eyes. The lynx snapped and snarled, pulling hard on its lead as it tried to get her.

"There you are," Scratch said with a satisfied hiss.

20

AN AUDIENCE WITH
HIS ROYAL EXCELLENCY

The emperor's throne didn't look particularly comfortable. It was made from an enormous black rock with huge crystalline spikes that stabbed out in all directions. If it wasn't for the emperor sitting on it, with his lynx at his feet, Casey would have assumed it was a torture device.

The throne was raised on a plinth in the centre of a richly decorated room. Casey wondered if the throne was always here, or if it was especially brought in from the emperor's shuttle. Maybe he had more than one? Or perhaps some unlucky Red Eyes had the job of carrying it wherever he went. It looked rather heavy.

She realized her mind was racing. It must be the adrenaline. She tried to calm herself as she watched the emperor confer with two of his overseers. He paid her no attention as she knelt on the floor at the base of his throne, forced to her knees by the imperial guards. The lynx kept its eyes on her warily, as if it expected her to turn invisible again at any moment.

A door opened on the left, just in her line of sight, and Scratch entered, escorting Pete and Xander.

"Pete!" Casey yelled in disbelief. She wanted to run over, but the imperial guards pushed her back down. Her brother looked at her in surprise.

"They told me you weren't coming," he said in a small, broken voice that barely registered in the high-ceilinged room. "What are you doing here?"

"We were trying to free the gamers," Casey said, uncertain how much she should say in front of the Arcturians. "I thought I could rescue everyone."

"How's that working out for you?" Xander asked. He flicked his fringe out of his eyes and whispered something to Pete that Casey couldn't hear. Pete glanced at Casey again. He looked embarrassed.

"What are *you* doing here?" she asked her brother uneasily. Something was wrong, she could tell.

"I'm sorry," Pete mumbled. "Fish said you were still on Hosin. I thought you weren't coming. I thought I was all on my own!"

Casey paused, sensing there was more to this

than she realized. "Oh my God, Pete! What have you done?"

"Your brother has made a deal," Xander said proudly, draping his arm across the boy's shoulders. "He has information they need. Valuable information. We're getting safe passage back to Earth."

Casey's eyes widened. "Information about what?"

"The one thing the Red Eyes want," Xander told her. "While you've been running around causing chaos, we've been negotiating a deal. A deal where everybody gets to go home."

There was a sudden growl from the plinth. The lynx bared its teeth them. They all fell silent. The emperor waited a moment, letting the stillness hang over the room ominously before he stood and approached them.

"So, this," he said, looking directly at Casey, "is the infamous human known as **CASEY_FLOW**. I expected you to be more ... *impressive*." His translator rendered his Arcturian into English for her benefit, even saying the underscore in her gamertag.

Scratch snorted, amused at the put-down. The imperial leader glared at her, irritated by the interruption. The ruff of skin around his neck puffed up in annoyance.

"I am surprised that a mere child has caused my

soldiers so much trouble both on Earth and on Hosin," the emperor continued. Scratch bowed her head at that rebuke, shooting Casey a look of intense hatred as she did so.

The emperor regarded Casey a moment. "While you have been interfering in our plans, your brother has proved surprisingly helpful. He has alerted us to the true location of the Squid array."

Casey looked at Pete. "You're working with them? You can't! If they get the array, they'll be unstoppable. They'll take over every planet in the galaxy. Including ours!"

Pete refused to meet her gaze.

"Earth will be safe," Xander said, flashing that charming yet somehow chilling smile of his. "We've negotiated a guarantee."

"Of course they'll invade the Earth!" Casey yelled. "It's what they do. It's all they do. The Squids told me they've taken over planet after planet."

"And you believed them?" Xander scoffed. "The Squids got inside your head and turned you around, Casey. They're the bad guys, not the Red—"

The lynx growled and Xander caught himself. He bowed to the emperor. "Excuse me, Your Highness, I meant, not the *Arcturians*."

"But what about the Squids? And the gamers? What will happen to them?" Casey demanded.

"Every negotiation comes with a price," the emperor told her, as the translation device caught up with the conversation. "Thanks to your brother we know that the psionic array is on Earth."

"On Earth?" Casey said, surprised. "But I thought it was on Hosin."

"So did we," the emperor said with a mirthless laugh. "But we have verified your brother's information and, with his help, we intend to—"

"Wait!" Casey interrupted, a feeling of dread sweeping over her. "How did you verify it?"

The lynx hissed at her as if affronted by her rudeness.

"It took a while, but the Bactu who brought you here was most talkative," the emperor said. The ruff of skin around his neck fluttered horribly. "Do you know, in all our history, we've never been able to capture and interrogate a live one. It was most illuminating."

"If you've hurt Eldreth—" Casey began.

The emperor cut her off with a wave of his hand then returned to his throne. "The Bactu have nothing left to offer us," he said as he retook his seat. "They will be removed from the negotiating table. Permanently."

Casey fought to get up off the floor. She wanted to fly at the emperor and wipe the smug look off his reptilian face. But the imperial guards shoved her back onto her knees. She saw Scratch watching her, enjoying every moment.

"The only question that remains is: what should we do with you?" the emperor mused, staring at Casey.

"Your Excellency," Scratch rasped. "This human girl has been nothing but a hindrance. She needs to be made an example of."

The emperor was clearly displeased by the interruption. Casey realized, for the first time, just how low down the Arcturian pecking order Scratch came. She was nothing more than a grunt. No wonder she'd been so angry at losing her promotion to overseer.

"And what would you suggest, Squad Sergeant? Should we send her back to Hosin? Or throw her into space?" The emperor spoke in Arcturian but the translator automatically rendered it into English.

"I see no reason why Your Excellency should be bothered by such a minor detail," Scratch said, bowing again. "I would like to deal with her myself. Our customs allow for personal enmities to be resolved in combat."

"You would fight a child?"

"She is more than that, Your Excellency."

The emperor turned to an overseer. "Have we ordered the retreat from Hosin?"

"Yes, Exalted One," the overseer replied, bowing so low her face was invisible beneath her hood. "The human gamers are being evacuated and placed into hibernation onboard the dropships. It will be a few hours until all our ships are ready to depart for Earth."

"Then there is nothing to do but wait," the emperor said, dismissing the overseer with a nod.

Casey realized that their plan to cut the signal would never have worked. Pete's decision to negotiate with the Arcturians had ruined everything. Because of him, the gamers had been ordered to retreat before she could free them from the Red Eyes' mind control. And because of him the Earth itself was now in danger. She cursed her little brother and that stupid, arrogant YouTuber who clearly had him twisted around his little finger.

"My troops have fought hard against the Bactu," the emperor announced. "They deserve a reward. A distraction to occupy them while we wait." He looked at Casey and smiled thinly. "I suggest an event."

"What kind of event, Exalted One?" an overseer asked. Everyone was so terrified of this regal reptilian,

Casey thought. It was the total opposite of Hosin, where the Squids seemed to live as equals.

"Let the Squad Sergeant have her duel," the emperor said. "It will provide entertainment for our troops while they await our inevitable victory."

Scratch's forked tongue flicked over her lips. "As you command, Your Excellency. Nothing would give me greater pleasure than to defeat an enemy of Arcturia."

"You want us to fight?" Casey asked, incredulous.

"It is a noble tradition on our home planet, Arcturia," the emperor said. "Only in combat can glory be won or lost."

"What do I get if I win?" Casey asked. The defiance in her voice surprised her more than anyone.

The emperor's smile was full of malice. His lips curled back to reveal a double row of lizard teeth, cracked and grey like ancient gravestones. "*If* you win, we will discuss the fate of your 'gamer' friends after we reach Earth." He turned to his overseers. "Put her in the Crucible. We shall be entertained."

The overseers bowed and scraped. The imperial guards hauled Casey to her feet and escorted her towards the doors.

"How could you make a deal with them?" Casey

hissed at Pete as she was pushed past him.

"Because it's the only way to get home! Your way failed. I didn't even know if you were coming back for me. I had to do something."

The words stung Casey like a slap.

"You can't blame the kid for your mistakes," Xander told her, a sly smile playing over his lips. Casey cursed herself. Xander was right. She'd abandoned Pete on Hosin and she hadn't told him what her plan was, not even when she'd got onto the space station. No wonder he'd given the Red Eyes what they wanted. He didn't know what else to do.

She felt Scratch's breath, hot and fetid, on her cheek.

"Don't worry, child," the alien said. "All this pain will end in the Crucible. I will make it swift."

21

BREAD AND CIRCUSES

Casey knew, from *SkyWake*'s lore, that combat was at the heart of Arcturian culture. The Red Eyes believed that only the strongest and deadliest fighters were fit to be leaders. Violence, and its spectacle, was the glue that held their warrior society together. That was why the Crucible was the most important place in Arcturian society. Every city, every town, had one. Like the Roman Colosseum, they were brutal arenas where blood was shed for the glory of the combatants and the entertainment of the masses.

The Crucible on the space station was bigger and stranger than any she had seen in *SkyWake*. It was circular, like a bullfighting ring, and fitted with climbing rows of seats that stretched high up above it on all sides. In the centre of the arena hung a circular metal platform, a battle stage where the fighters would go head to head. What was terrifying, though, was that the platform wasn't set on solid ground. Instead, it was suspended above an enormous, seemingly bottomless chasm that stretched beneath it into darkness.

To enter the Crucible each fighter came through a set of doors and onto a narrow walkway that led across the chasm towards the battle stage. As Casey stepped out, she tried not to look down into the abyss below her feet. There was a click as the doors she'd just come through locked behind her. She realized there were only two ways out of the Crucible: as a victor, or in a body bag.

A roar of sound hit her as she took her first steps onto the walkway. She looked up to see hundreds of Red Eyes in the seats that encircled the arena. Grunts, pilots and ground crew were in the audience, all eager to watch the impending battle. Their reptilian faces, male and female, were marked with utter hatred for this human girl. The emperor was right. She was infamous.

Casey continued along the narrow walkway, trying to ignore the hollering and booing. It had no guard rails. There was, she realized with a flash of vertigo, nothing to stop her from falling into the chasm below. She put one foot in front of another, suddenly feeling off balance. As she reached the end, she noticed that it didn't actually connect to the battle stage. There was a yawning gap between her walkway and the stage itself. The gap was too far for her to jump, even with a run-up. Disconcerted, she stood there, balanced above the chasm, feeling like an unlucky sailor who'd been made to walk the plank.

She stared up at the watching audience of Red Eyes, sensing their bloodlust. Her deactivated infiltrator suit, its battery cells ripped out by her captors, clung tight to her skin. Even though she'd pulled the silver hood off her face, she felt like she was suffocating.

The emperor sat in an elevated seating box across the arena, perfectly positioned for a bird's-eye view of the action below. Beside him sat Pete and Xander. They looked more like his guests than prisoners.

Casey wondered where her teammates were. Brain, Elite and Dreyfus must be being held captive somewhere on the station. Was Fish now with them? Was Cheeze still in the shuttle? Or had he been discovered? And what about Eldreth? She hadn't seen the Squid since he'd gone to negotiate Hosin's surrender. The emperor said they'd interrogated him. Had they hurt him? Her team, she realized with a jolt, had been ripped apart and it was all her fault. Her choices – no, her *mistakes* – had led them to this point. She should never have suggested splitting the group back on the beach. Nor should she have ignored Xolotl's offer of help. She'd been so stupid, convinced she knew what she was doing when she really didn't know anything at all.

On the other side of the Crucible, a door slid open and Scratch emerged. The alien, wearing an orange jumpsuit instead of her usual chunky black power armour, strode onto her walkway with a confident step. When she reached the end of it she raised her fist to the watching crowd and clamped it to her chest in a salute and then she bowed low to the emperor. The Red Eyes went wild, roaring with approval. Scratch jumped up and down a few times on the edge of the walkway and twisted her neck in a circle, limbering up.

The emperor stood and the crowd fell silent. He paused for dramatic effect before he spoke. Casey couldn't understand the words, but she didn't need to. It was obvious that he was prepping them for the coming battle, explaining the terms of the deal that had been struck. The two contestants were here to fight for their lives. If Casey won, she would have a chance of freeing the gamers. But if she lost, she'd... What? Be taken prisoner? Die? She wasn't sure. The idea of losing her life here, light years from home, as Pete looked on, made her tremble. It was too much. She thought of her dad dying in a dusty street in Afghanistan. Had he felt like this too? It seemed so cruel, so unfair.

While the emperor continued to speak, Casey composed herself. She took advantage of the distraction to familiarize herself with the arena. If she was going to fight here, she needed to know the terrain.

One look convinced her that the place was a death trap. To reach the main battle stage she would have to jump from her walkway onto one of three floating platforms that circled around the stage in a slow, clockwise motion. Then she would have to time a second jump onto the battle stage, avoiding the spiked traps that lined the edges. The whole thing reminded her of a *Super Smash Bros.* arena.

On the upside, each floating platform held a weapons crate. Perhaps, she thought drily, they might hold a power-up. A Bullet Bill or a Poké Ball would come in handy right about now. She sighed and pulled her hair back from her face and tied it into a ponytail to keep it out of her eyes. The prospect of facing Scratch in battle was no joke.

One thing confused her about the layout of the arena. Normally there were only two fighters in the Crucible. But here there were three walkways. What, or who, was the third one for? No sooner had she wondered this than there came a low rumble and the doors leading onto it slid open. The arena fell still in excited anticipation. A new fighter had arrived.

Casey gasped as Eldreth slithered out onto the third walkway, ducking his bulbous head low to squeeze through the entrance. At the sight of the Bactu, the crowd erupted, booing and jeering in disgust. The Squid looked completely different from when Casey had last seen him, barely an hour ago. His body was bruised and battered, covered in bloody wounds from where he'd been tortured. Several implants had been inserted into his head, piercing his translucent skin. A thick band of black metal stretched across his forehead like a belt, squeezing his flesh, searing into it. His large grey eyes were unfocussed and confused and, as he moved across the walkway on his tentacles, Casey could see he was in pain. He looked defeated and lost.

"Eldreth!" Casey shouted across the gap between them. "What have they done to you?" She expected to feel the Squid's presence sneak into her mind, but it didn't come. The Red Eye device on his head must be interfering with his psi powers.

The Squid turned to look at her, his eyes mournful.

"I was right about you humans," he said, speaking

aloud in English in his birdlike voice. "You gave the Arcturians everything they needed."

"We can still win this!"

"I won't take part in this ridiculous spectacle," the Squid replied, shaking his head. "There is nothing left to fight for. They've already won." His body sagged, exhausted and broken. Before Casey could respond, the emperor shouted something to the crowd in Arcturian, and the arena erupted in excitement.

The fight, she realized with a jolt, had begun.

Scratch moved first, sprinting along her walkway and leaping over the chasm onto one of the floating platforms as it circled past. She made the jump with perfect timing, clearly a veteran of this place. Then she tore open the weapons crate on the floating platform and pulled out an energy sword, brandishing it in the air triumphantly. The crowd went wild as she fired it up, its blade shimmering and vicious.

Casey, a few seconds behind, sprinted to the end of her own walkway. But she missed her chance to jump onto the first floating platform. It sailed past, leaving her teetering on the edge, trying not to look into the chasm below her. She willed the next floating platform to hurry as it circled around towards her. Just before it arrived, she took a few steps back, did another run-up and leaped across to it. Her stomach flipped as she saw the bottomless blackness beneath her.

Landing on the floating platform, she rushed to the weapons crate. The Arcturian electronic lock was strange and unfamiliar, unlike anything she'd seen in *SkyWake*. As she hammered the crate's touchscreen, she looked up to see Scratch barrelling towards her across the main battle stage. The alien was getting ready to jump onto Casey's platform, an Arcturian battle cry roaring from her mouth. The crowd cheered, impressed by this proactive display. Killing your enemy before they even made it onto the main battle stage was a rare occurrence.

Casey ducked as the Red Eye landed in front of her, dodging the energy sword as it swung towards her head. The blade sliced into the weapons crate, destroying it and whatever was inside it. Casey rolled, desperately trying not to fall off the floating platform, then pulled herself onto her feet and leaped across to the main stage. Her infiltrator suit snagged on the spiked traps, tearing a huge gash in her leg. A line of blood dripped down her calf.

Behind her, Scratch howled in annoyance. The alien had to wait until the floating platform circled around to the next opening between the spikes on the main stage before she could give chase. Casey made the most of the few valuable seconds she'd won and sprinted forward to put some distance between her and her enemy.

The battle stage was dotted with obstacles – rope nets, pitfall traps and even a web of laser beams. The aim was to cause as much injury and mayhem as possible. It was like the set of a reality TV show, Casey thought. *I'm a Celebrity... Get Me Out of Here!* but in space with homicidal aliens.

In the centre of the arena, surrounded by the lasers, stood a plinth that held a purple crate. Casey wanted a weapon in her hand more than anything. The crate's position, right in the middle of the Crucible and defended by the deadly beams, convinced her it must contain something worth having. She hoped it was a plasma rifle.

She ran towards it, sliding low beneath the first set of waist-high beams and then crawling on her belly under the rest. To her surprise, the crate clicked open first time. Over her shoulder she could see Scratch leaping across to the main battle stage with her energy sword in her hand. Eldreth was still standing on his walkway. He hadn't moved at all. He'd clearly given up.

Sensing an immense fight was about to erupt, the watching Red Eyes jumped to their feet, cheering and hollering. Casey reached into the crate and pulled out something hard and metal. She stared at it. It was an energy shield baton.

"A shield?" she yelled, outraged. "What am I supposed to do with a *shield*?" She wanted to scream in despair. She needed a weapon. A plasma rifle or an energy sword. Heck, even a bow and arrow would do.

Scratch appeared behind her, slashing through the lattice of laser beams with her sword, effortlessly destroying them. Then she charged onto the plinth, whirling the blade above her head like some kind of samurai warrior. Casey dodged, her fingers fumbling over the shield baton as she tried to work out how to use it. She'd never played as a tank in *SkyWake*, and the tech was strange and unfamiliar.

She looked up at the emperor's box, hoping to catch a glimpse of her little brother. Maybe he could tell her what to do with it. But when her eyes fell on Pete's seat, she gasped.

It was empty.

She didn't have time to question what this meant. A voice behind her chilled her blood.

"It's time to end this, Cay See," Scratch sneered.

Then she swung her energy sword in a wide arc at the defenceless girl's head. Casey dived left, hitting the floor hard. She looked up from the ground to see Scratch standing over her. The blade of light crackled, ready to bring the fight to an end.

22

FOLLOW THAT DRONE

Pete watched the fight, appalled. He didn't know what he had expected, but it hadn't been this. It was so vicious and brutal.

He glanced at Xander and the emperor, noticing how the YouTuber was doing his best to ingratiate himself with the Arcturian leader. The way Xander had negotiated the deal had been masterful. He'd even convinced the emperor that the Arcturians would need Xander and Pete on Earth to act as their guides.

Xander, Pete decided, was a survivor. Casey was a survivor too, but a different kind. She was stubborn and unwilling to yield, whereas Xander changed course whenever it suited him. It was like what Pete's dad used to say about martial arts. Boxing and karate relied on force: smash, hit, whack. Jiu-jitsu was more like a dance where you used your attacker's weight and momentum against them. Xander was definitely a dancer. Casey, Pete decided, not so much. She was more like a hammer in search of a nail.

He wondered why she was so determined to keep on fighting. It was clear she couldn't win. Xander had negotiated a deal that could save them. Why couldn't Casey just go along with it? Why did she care so much about the freaky-looking Squids? Whatever was happening between the Squids and the Red Eyes, it wasn't her fight.

Pete just hoped that Scratch would end the battle quickly. Kill the Squid and force Casey to surrender. His throat caught. That *was* what would happen, wasn't it? Xander had promised him that this fight was just for show. But watching Casey in the arena, Pete began to worry. What if she didn't surrender? What if she was stubborn? Would the Red Eyes respect the deal they'd made? Or would they simply cut her loose?

He felt a sudden urge to throw up. He stumbled out of his seat, unnoticed by Xander or the Red Eyes in the emperor's box. The lynx stared at him lazily then looked away. It didn't think he was even worth a growl.

In the corridor behind the seating area, Pete leaned against the wall, steadying himself with one arm. He felt faint and a little panicky. He heard the crowd roar with delight in the arena as the contest continued.

As he stood there, trying not to hurl, he saw a drone sail along the far end of the corridor. He thought nothing of it. There were always lots of drones on the space station. They were programmed to keep the place running smoothly, making repairs and overseeing the various systems. But something about the way it moved, hesitant and uncertain, caught his attention.

It looked like it was lost.

Which was weird.

How could a drone be lost?

He watched as it hovered in the middle of the corridor, wobbling slightly as if its gyroscope was malfunctioning. Noticing him, it chirruped excitedly and approached, the lights on its chassis flickering like a Christmas tree. It twirled around in mid-air in a barrel roll and then dived between his legs. Pete stared in surprise. He'd never seen an Arcturian drone act like this. They were normally focussed on whatever mission they'd been programmed to complete. But this one was like a playful puppy. It stared at him with its fisheye lens and then chirruped at him insistently.

"Are you trying to talk to me?" Pete asked. The drone bobbed up and down and flashed its lights on and off in a fast-paced sequence. "I don't understand what you're trying to say."

"What the hell are you doing, kid?" Xander's voice was tetchy. Pete spun around to see the YouTuber glaring at him angrily. "Are you trying to mess up everything?"

"I just needed some air," Pete said. "But then I saw this drone. I think it's … I dunno, like, lost or something."

Xander gave the drone a contemptuous glance. "Get out of here!" he ordered, waving it away. The drone bobbed in the air. Xander batted it with his hands. It dodged him. "Stupid piece of junk doesn't understand English." He turned back to Pete. "We need to get back to the arena before the Red Eyes notice we're gone. Otherwise—"

BZZT!

"Ow!" Xander yelled, rubbing his arm. "That thing just shocked me!"

The drone retracted its extendable arm, then chirruped and flew off down the corridor bobbing and weaving unsteadily.

"I think it's trying to tell us something," Pete said. "C'mon, let's follow it!" Casey's fight temporarily forgotten, he set off down the corridor after the drone.

Xander trailed behind him, grumbling.

The corridors were eerie and deserted. All the Red Eyes were either prepping for the journey to Earth or watching the fight in the arena. As they followed the drone down several levels, Pete recognized the signs on the walls. They were heading back towards the prison block. He paused, worried about causing trouble. Maybe Xander was right. The drone stopped too and then, as if sensing his hesitation, it flew around his waist before swooping between his legs, encouraging him to keep following.

"It must have short-circuited," Xander sniffed. "Let's leave it and get back."

"No, it's definitely up to something," Pete said, eyeing it. "I think it's something to do with the Reapers."

Xander frowned. "Those idiots! If they interfere, they'll ruin everything!"

"Shouldn't we help them?"

"Are you nuts?" Xander said. "Five kids can't take on a whole alien army. We need to be smart and take the deal. It's the only way. You have something the Red Eyes want. We can use that to get what *we* want too."

Pete was swayed by his logic. He wanted to be home. Everything Casey and her team were doing seemed to be making the Arcturians angrier. He watched as the drone disappeared around a corner into the prison block. As it did, two more appeared and flanked it like bodyguards.

Xander's brow furrowed. "Hmm. You're right. Something is going on. Let's take a look."

The two boys hung back behind the corner and watched cautiously as the drones sailed into the prison block. The Arcturian guards standing on duty at the entrance, used to seeing drones going about their business, paid them no attention.

That was a mistake. As soon as the drones had passed the guards, two of them spun around noiselessly, floated up behind the Red Eyes and delivered a powerful shock to the backs of their necks. The soldiers crumpled to the floor.

Meanwhile, the third drone headed over to a computer terminal outside the boys' cell and patched into the prison block's systems with a series of shrill beeps. A moment later, the energy field over the cells deactivated. Brain, Elite and Fish cautiously stepped out and looked around in surprise. They grinned with delight as they saw the comatose bodies of the Red Eye guards.

Pete almost shouted when he saw his sister's

teammates, but Xander shushed him, putting a finger to his lips. The two of them waited, hidden behind the corner, and watched in silence as the Ghost Reapers approached the drones.

"Cheeze?" Brain asked, peering into the lens of the lead drone. "Is that you?"

The machine whistled and then did a flip in the air.

"Cheeze by name, cheesy by nature!" Fish smirked. He patted the drone as if it was a pet dog. "Thanks for the jailbreak."

"We need to find Casey," Elite said, looking into the drone's front camera lens. "Do you know where she is, bruv?" The drone whistled an affirmative.

From his hiding place, Pete felt a stab of jealousy. These guys had such a good rapport. They were more than just teammates. They were mate mates.

"Shouldn't we tell them what's going on?" he asked Xander quietly. He thought of the danger Casey was in back at the Crucible.

The YouTuber's grip on his arm tightened. "Don't be silly, kid. We've got to stick to our plan. Let's just wait and find out what they're up to."

Pete watched as Dreyfus and Private Ross followed the boys out of the cell.

"How do we get off the station?" Fish asked. "Eldreth said there was some kind of tractor beam pulling in our shuttle when we arrived. If we don't disable it, the shuttle can't escape. They'll catch us and suck us back up again like a Hoover."

Private Ross stared at the downed Red Eye guards, unable to believe he was finally free. Dreyfus grabbed a couple of plasma rifles from their unconscious hands. He passed one to the private. "Do you know the layout of this place?" he asked.

The young soldier smiled, pleased to be of use. "I designed a space station level for *SkyWake*, I know these corridors like the back of my hand."

"Outstanding." Dreyfus nodded, then turned to the boys. "Private Ross and I will deal with this space Hoover thing. The rest of you need to rescue Casey and the giant squid. We'll meet you in the docking bay."

Pete gulped. No one, it seemed, was thinking about rescuing *him*.

"How will you get to the ship?" Brain asked.

"Old soldiers know how to take care of themselves," Dreyfus said and turned to Private Ross. "Don't we, son?"

"You got it, LT."

They were like a father and son discussing a fishing trip.

"You guys look after yourselves," Private Ross told the boys, giving them a tight salute.

Pete felt Xander's grip relax on his arm.

"Doesn't look like they give a damn about us, does it?" the YouTuber said, voicing Pete's own thoughts. "We need to tell the Arcturians what's going on before those idiots spoil everything. C'mon!" He turned and headed back down the corridor.

Pete paused, sensing it was time to choose a side. But, really, he thought to himself, the decision had already been made. If no one cared about him, then Xander was right.

He had to look out for himself.

23

DON'T HANG AROUND

Scratch stood over Casey, her energy sword pointing at the girl's chest. The roar of the Red Eyes in the arena had reached a fever pitch. They were baying for blood.

"You have been a worthy opponent," Scratch said, the translation device on her jumpsuit picking up speed to keep up with her words, "but this is where it ends."

"It's not over yet," Casey said, fighting to catch her breath. "The Squids will stop you." She kept her eyes on Scratch while her fingers fumbled over the shield baton, trying to activate it.

Scratch knelt, bringing her face close to Casey's. The crowd roared on.

"Oh, but they can't," the alien said, her ugly mouth twitching with delight as the translator rendered her words in English. "Don't you understand, girl? Hosin is of no importance any more. It's gone."

"What do you mean?" Casey asked, her stomach sinking.

"We know the array is on Earth. Your 'Pete' will help us locate it. Hosin has served its purpose. It is no longer needed."

The alien paused and Casey realized Scratch was keeping something from her. She scrabbled at the baton's buttons again, trying to find the right combination.

"What are you going to do to the Squids?"

"It's already done. Our fleet has launched a planet-killing bomb. Hosin will be obliterated."

"You can't wipe out an entire planet!" Casey cried.

"It isn't the first … and it won't be the last." Scratch grinned and tightened her grip on the energy sword, preparing to finish this. That was when Casey finally noticed that the arena had fallen silent. The Red Eyes were no longer cheering. Scratch sensed it at the same moment. She looked over her shoulder to see Eldreth slithering towards them. The Squid had finally roused himself to join the fight. He had leaped onto the main battle stage and approached without either of them seeing him.

He snapped a tentacle towards Scratch in a vicious

attack, while another wrapped itself around Casey's waist and pulled her to safety.

Furious, Scratch sliced the incoming tentacle with her blade. It fell to the floor, twitching. The Squid yelled in pain and Casey found herself spinning across the arena floor as Eldreth released her from his grip. She clung tightly to the shield baton.

The two aliens faced off against each other, Squid tentacles versus energy sword. Eldreth was big and heavy, and without his psi powers he had no chance of winning. Scratch danced around him with a fighter's poise, ducking under his tentacles and slashing at them with her blade. Eldreth screamed as Scratch seared first one and then another limb from his body, before spinning around to deliver a slash across the Squid's flank.

A moment later, Casey saw Eldreth's body sag and his remaining tentacles droop as he collapsed to the floor. The blade severed the metal band around his head and a torrent of blood, the colour of algae, flowed from his wounds.

Scratch held her sword aloft as she prepared to deliver the *coup de grâce*.

"It's time for the caretakers to step aside," she shouted, playing to the crowd. "Arcturia is ascendant!"

The arena erupted with cheers of excitement.

She drove her sword down towards the Squid's prone body. But the blade stopped before it could reach its intended victim. Casey had finally activated the energy shield, hitting the right combination of buttons as much by chance as anything else. She stepped in front of the falling sword and the weapon glanced off her shield with an exasperated crackle of dissipated energy. The device was smaller than Fish's energy barrier – it was a personal shield rather than a squad one – but it did the job.

Scratch howled with rage and Casey braced herself as the alien's sword struck again and again, raining down blows on her shield. She put one leg out behind her, steadying herself as she'd seen Fish do when he played tank. Scratch slashed and hacked at the shield. The watching Red Eyes bellowed, angry that their bloodlust remained unsated.

The shield held and Scratch paused to catch her breath, muttering curses as she tried to work out how to get past her opponent. Casey, glad for a moment's respite from the blows, prepared herself for a fresh attack.

You saved me, Eldreth said, his voice sneaking back in her mind now that the metal headband had been broken. The Squid seemed weak and sickly.

"Someone had to show you humans weren't immature," Casey said, looking at him over her shoulder. The blood from Eldreth's wounds was spreading across the floor. "Tell me what to do. Can you use your psi powers to fight back?"

I'm dying, Casey.

The simplicity of his words hit her hard. "You can't!" she cried. "They've launched a bomb at Hosin, and I still have to rescue Pete and the others. I need you, Eldreth."

Like I told you, sometimes it's not possible to win without sacrificing something.

"But I don't know what I'm doing. I don't know what choices to make. I don't know how to lead."

You're a caretaker, Casey. You look after others and do your best to help them, just like the Bactu. You know what to do. You just have to ... go with the flow.

"Eldreth, please—"

She felt Eldreth's presence suddenly recede from her mind and realized, looking at the Squid's motionless body, that he was gone for ever. Scratch's blade had done its evil work. The arena erupted in cheers as the watching Red Eyes celebrated their comrade's victory.

Casey didn't have time to grieve. Scratch's energy sword flew towards her as the alien launched yet another blistering attack. The human girl braced herself, willing her shield to absorb the blows. Without a way to fight back, though, she knew she was just postponing the inevitable. Her shield was already beginning to crack as it drew the last of the power from the baton's battery cells.

With a final roar, Scratch took her sword in two hands and brought it down, hard, onto the shield. The barrier splintered apart, fragments of pure energy falling onto the floor and then vanishing like embers from a fire. Casey felt the heat of the sword as it sliced through the air beside her, just missing her arm. She rolled to one side, trying to get away before Scratch could strike again. As she did, the floor vanished beneath her.

She'd rolled off the edge!

She grabbed the lip of the stage with both hands as she fell, clinging on to it with all her strength. She felt the pull of gravity beneath her and, looking down, stared into the dark pit beyond her dangling feet. The pit was so dark, it seemed to swallow the light. It would swallow her, too, the moment she let go. She knew it wouldn't be more than a few seconds. The pain in her arms from holding on was beyond anything she'd ever felt, a screaming red-hot agony that took her breath away.

Flushed with her victory over the Squid, Scratch sneered down at Casey. She hissed mockingly at her. "She hisses," the translation device said, helpful as ever.

"You fought well, girl. You will die with honour and glory. Do you have any last words?"

"Stuff you, you brain-dead space lizard!" Casey yelled, raging with anger and despair. Scratch's eyes blinked sideways as the translation device struggled to render the words in Arcturian. Realizing it was an insult, Scratch snarled and brought her heavy combat boot crunching down onto Casey's left hand. The girl screamed and lost her grip. Pain shot through her body as she struggled to hold on with just her right hand. The watching Red Eyes hollered and pumped the air with their fists, savouring every second. Scratch's humiliation in the shopping centre was now forgotten.

Scratch raised her boot again, ready to finish this. She looked to the emperor, seeking his approval. Casey, gasping with the exertion of hanging off the lip of the stage, followed the alien's gaze. To her surprise, she saw the emperor talking animatedly to Xander, who had now reappeared in the arena. Something was happening. She searched the stands for Pete but she couldn't see him anywhere.

She wished more than anything that she could feel that power rising inside her again. Where was it when she needed it? Why wasn't it coming? How could she go with the flow when she couldn't feel anything at all?

Tears streaked down her face. Tears of pain but also of despair. Eldreth was dead. Pete was gone. The Reapers had split apart. The Red Eyes had found the array and Hosin was about to be obliterated.

It was over.

And it was all her fault.

She looked up at Scratch. The alien's eyes flashed with spite as she prepared to crush Casey beneath her boot as if she was nothing more than a troublesome bug.

"Goodbye, Cay See," the alien said in faltering English.

Before Scratch could bring her boot down to finish her, though, Casey let go of the ledge. It was a tiny act of defiance, her only way of thwarting the vindictive Red Eye's victory. She felt her body drop like a stone into the chasm below her.

As she tumbled through the air, the stage receded above her until it was nothing but a pinprick of light. The last thing she saw was Scratch standing on the edge of it, shaking her energy sword in the air, furious at having been denied the chance to kill her.

Casey fell down, down, down. The chasm's darkness engulfed her. She closed her eyes waiting for the inevitable end.

That was when she heard the drones.

They approached in formation, a dozen of them at least, bunched together and racing across the pit to intercept her fall. As they surrounded her, a force field extended between them like a giant net. She dropped into it. It was soft and springy, like a trampoline.

The drones bobbed up and down in mid-air as their servomotors strained to take her weight. With effort they lifted her prone body towards the side of the chasm. A service hatch opened as they approached.

Before Casey knew what was happening, the drones had deposited her inside the safety of a metal vent. She lay there, stunned, as the drones flew back out the hatch and ascended into the arena. One drone stayed behind as if to check she was all right. It hovered beside her, its fisheye lens reflecting her own face back to her.

"Thank you, Cheeze," she said gratefully, guessing who was behind her rescue. She gave the drone a gentle pat. It beeped at her in delight and then headed up to join its friends.

24

THE TROLLEY PROBLEM
... IN SPACE?

The space station was in chaos. Drones whizzed along the corridors, attacking any Red Eyes they saw. Alarms blared as the Arcturians, stumbling out of the arena, realized they were under attack. Hundreds of Cheeze's drones swooped down, like angry mechanical mosquitoes, zapping them mercilessly.

As Casey emerged from a vent, she had to duck to avoid a blast of plasma fire. The Red Eye grunts were fighting back against the drones, or at least those that could were. Most of the soldiers were unarmed, having come straight from the arena. Their joy at Scratch's victory turned sour as they found themselves scurrying for cover from their own tech.

Casey stumbled through the chaos. The drones, programmed to ignore her, paid her no attention.

One grunt grabbed her arm as she headed towards the docking bay, shouting something indecipherable in Arcturian at her. However, he was quickly forced to let go when a pack of drones swarmed down on him.

Free again, Casey sprinted ahead, bobbing and weaving through the plasma fire. She was almost at the docking bay when she saw Brain, Elite and Fish running towards her.

"Casey!" Brain cried, giving her a rare smile. "You made it!"

"Only thanks to Cheeze."

"Us too," Fish grinned. "I swear that boy can hack anything."

"Are you hurt?" Brain asked, seeing Casey's bruised hand and the deep gash down her leg.

A stray plasma burst hit the wall beside her before she could respond. There was no time to talk. The reunited Reapers sprinted into the docking bay. The shuttle was where they'd left it earlier, but their path was now blocked by three squads of Red Eyes who were fighting off the drones with some success.

"What do we do?" Casey yelled. There was no way to get past the grunts. As if in answer to her question, a figure appeared on the ramp of the shuttle. It was Cheeze, sitting in a bulky wheelchair that seemed to hover in mid-air. It had clearly been bolted together using scavenged parts – a padded seat from the bridge, a computer terminal ripped from the shuttle's console, and an anti-grav propulsion system. Instead of wheels, it had two metal discs that hovered above the ground.

"Whoa!" Elite whistled, impressed. "Cheeze got himself a new ride!"

Their friend steered his chair towards them, dodging a path through the battling drones and Red Eyes.

"I upgraded," he said, grinning in pride as he pulled up beside them. "Say hello to wheelchair 2.0." He spun the hoverchair around in a nifty 360. "So much better than that power armour."

Before they could say any more, a drone, blasted by plasma fire, flew out of the air and crashed to the ground beside them in a shower of sparks.

"Everyone get behind me!" Cheeze said, tapping a touchscreen mounted on his chair.

"Hey, that's my line," Fish huffed, but he obeyed nonetheless.

A shield sprang up in front of the hoverchair and the Reapers stayed close as Cheeze led them towards the shuttle. Two Red Eyes went to stop them, but Cheeze unleashed plasma fire from a rifle attached to the chair's side.

"This thing is like a tank!" Elite yelled in excitement, punching Fish on the arm. "It's gonna put you out of business, bruv!"

By the time the Reapers made it to the shuttle's ramp, drones were falling out of the air one after another, blasted by the Red Eyes' guns. The aliens were turning the tide against the hacked machines. The teammates ran into the shuttle and Cheeze reversed up the ramp after them, shielding his friends from enemy fire before sealing the shuttle tight.

While Cheeze readied the engines, the rest of the Reapers crowded around the bridge. The main navigational display, a 3D hologram that flickered in the air, showed their position in space. They could see the space station they were on, plus Hosin and the solar system's two distant suns. A huge projectile, as big as a spaceship, was making its way across the gap between the space station and the planet. The indicator on the display flashed ominously, blinking on and off like a fire alarm.

"That's the bomb ship the Red Eyes launched," Casey explained to the others, pointing. "They're trying to wipe out Hosin." Her finger poked right through the hologram, making it flicker. If only it was that easy to knock the real thing off course.

"Are we going to stop it?" Cheeze asked. "In a few minutes it'll be too far away for us to catch."

"We *have* to stop it," Casey replied. "We can't just watch them destroy an entire planet." She looked around the bridge, realizing they were missing someone. "Where's the lieutenant?"

"He went to turn off the tractor beam," Brain explained. "So we can get away. He found an old comrade of his, the guy who designed *SkyWake*."

No sooner had he said it than the main screen flashed into life with an incoming broadcast. Dreyfus's face filled the screen, close up and in high definition. He was in the tractor beam control room holding back two squads of Red Eye grunts while Private Ross worked on a terminal. It looked like they were about to be overrun.

Casey stared at the younger soldier. It was hard to believe he was the man behind *SkyWake*. She was glad Dreyfus had found him, though. She knew the lieutenant had always blamed himself for letting him be abducted by the aliens.

"Lieutenant? Can you hear us?" Cheeze asked, speaking to the screen. "We made it to the shuttle. How are you doing with turning off the tractor beam?"

Dreyfus didn't have time to chat. He shouted across

the room over the sound of plasma fire. "Private Ross! ETA?"

"Any second now, LT. Almost got it."

The Reapers watched the screen as a Red Eye opened fire at the soldiers. Dreyfus ducked. Casey saw he was already bleeding badly from a wound in his shoulder. Across the room, Private Ross yelped in pain as he was hit by flying shrapnel. He stayed at the main terminal, determined to finish the job. For the first time since the Ghost Reapers had met him, the soldier looked full of life. It was as if all his years in captivity had been forgotten. He was with his commanding officer again, fighting side by side.

"You're all clear!" he shouted as he finished the deactivation sequence.

"We won't be able to make it back to you," Dreyfus warned the Reapers. Private Ross ran over and dropped beside him, and the pair hunkered down behind the console as the Red Eyes continued to blast at them. "You'll have to take off without us."

Casey didn't want to listen. "We can't just leave you!"

"Use your drones to help them!" Fish urged Cheeze, grabbing the hacker's arm.

"They're down to seven per cent," he replied, looking at the display screens fitted onto his new wheelchair in despair. "There's not enough."

"We've got to try!"

"We'll buy you enough time to escape," Dreyfus called out, giving the Reapers a nod of encouragement via the comms screen. "Just make sure you stop the Red Eyes."

Back in the shuttle, the Reapers looked at one another, uncertain what to do.

"Ain't right leaving them behind like this," Elite said, shaking his head.

"If we're going to stop the bomb before it hits Hosin, we need to move," Cheeze said, one eye on the stream of data on the shuttle's screens. He was tracking the bomb's journey through space towards the planet below. "If we wait much longer, we won't have time to intercept it."

Nobody knew what to do. They were paralysed at the thought of having to make a decision like this under pressure. Should they abandon the soldiers, or wait for them and risk losing the chance to stop the bomb?

Just then, through the shuttle's main window, Casey saw movement across the docking bay. The emperor, flanked by his imperial guard, was heading over the bridge that spanned the bay. Scratch brought up the rear, leading Pete and Xander with her.

Casey stared at her little brother. He didn't look like a prisoner. There was no shock shackle around his neck. No one pushing him forward. He glanced down at the shuttle in the bay and caught sight of his sister through the reinforced-glass windshield. They locked eyes for a moment.

"Where he's going?" Cheeze asked, following her gaze. "Why isn't he coming with us?"

"He's with the Red Eyes now," Casey said flatly. "He's going to help them get what they want."

"This is all my fault, Casey," Fish muttered. "I let him think you weren't coming to rescue him. I was just trying to convince the Red Eyes you were still on Hosin, but Pete saw my whole act and I never got the chance to explain to him what was really going on."

On the main screen, the teammates could see the Red Eyes moving into the control room protected by a shield tank. The two human soldiers crouched together behind the comms terminal, overwhelmed by the amount of plasma fire being thrown at them. The boys stared in horror as the transmission continued.

"Thank you for coming back for me, sir," they heard Private Ross say to his commanding officer. Then his fingers moved quickly over the touchscreen of his plasma rifle. He looked into the comms screen, directly at the Reapers. "Like I said, it wasn't an exploit…"

The rifle hummed, drawing the remaining power from its battery packs. Its screen began to flash in a rapid warning. Private Ross had entered the self-destruct command, what *SkyWake* fans called the "shake 'n' bake".

"It's been an honour serving with you, Private," Dreyfus said. Then he turned to look at the comms screen. "Godspeed, Ghost Reapers."

With that the transmission cut and the screen went to black.

"We have to help them!" Fish shouted. "Casey, you go after your brother. We'll get to the lieutenant."

"We can't," Casey said firmly.

The boys stared, surprised at the steel in her voice.

"There isn't time. We'll never get to the control room before it's overrun and, even if we could, we can't save them and stop the bomb from destroying the Squids."

"But what about Pete?" Fish asked.

"He's made his own choices."

"There must be something we can do," Elite cried, pulling at his hair in desperation. "Think of something, brainiac!"

Brain shook his head, at a loss. He was out of ideas.

"That bomb is going to wipe out a whole planet, a whole species," Casey told them, feeling the weight of responsibility on their shoulders. "We have to stop it. Eldreth died to get us here."

"So, we're just going to abandon our friends and your brother, to save the Squids?" Fish demanded.

Hearing their decision laid out like that made Casey tremble. There wasn't a good solution. Every choice was a bad one. There was no way to save everyone.

"It's the trolley problem," she said.

"You can't make a call like that," Elite muttered.

"Someone has to," Cheeze chipped in, nodding at Casey supportively.

Fish shook his head in frustration. "I don't know what you think you're doing," he told Casey.

"I'm leading," she told him. "Because no one else wants to."

The boys fell silent. It was true. None of them were willing to take charge and make this dreadful decision. Casey was the only one who had stepped up. She turned to Cheeze. "Get us out of here before the tractor beam comes back online."

The shuttle's engines burst into life, lifting it off the docking bay's landing platform. A moment later, they flew out into deep space.

25

INFORMATION IS POWER

Pete stood on the observation deck on the space station and stared out at the vast inky canvas that stretched in all directions, searching for a sign of his sister.

He knew that she and the Reapers had managed to escape in a shuttle. The Red Eyes knew it too, although they didn't seem in any rush to go after them. They were focussed instead on getting ready to head to Earth.

Pete had no idea what Casey was planning to do out there in space, but he knew that she had made the wrong choice by choosing to fight. The Red Eyes were the only ones who could get them back to Earth. The Squids didn't even have any spaceships of their own. They seemed useless, apart from their psychic powers. He wished she'd stayed with him.

Xander's hand landed on his shoulder, startling him.

"You know, I have an older sister," the YouTuber told him, as if guessing the focus of Pete's thoughts. "She used to boss me around all the time. Like, 'Big sister knows best', you get what I mean?"

Pete knew exactly what he meant.

"She used to nag me about getting my A-levels and going to a good uni," Xander continued. "But now she's got her degree, she's in debt up to her eyeballs. She's had to move back home with our parents because she can't find a job. Meanwhile, I'm making proper bank from my streaming. I'm buying a city centre apartment. She hates it."

"I guess she's just jealous."

"Too right!"

"Maybe you could give her a job," Pete suggested. "With X-Squad, your company? She could be your assistant or something?"

Xander looked at him like he'd just grown a second head. "No way! When you win a fight, you've gotta savour it. You can't just go and cheapen a victory by turning your enemies into allies. At least, not until they beg you..." He grinned and pushed his fringe out of his eyes.

Pete fell silent, thinking more about Casey. Were *they* rivals? Casey had always competed with him for their dad's attention. She was the one who pretended to be interested in that stupid *Space Invaders* cabinet just to spend time with him. She was the one who'd tried to keep *SkyWake* to herself. She hadn't even invited him to join her clan. And since the invasion at the eSports tournament, she'd kept trying to be in charge: the big sister, the big leader.

Xander checked over his shoulder and then moved a little closer to Pete, his face sallow and serious.

"Listen, kid, the Red Eyes want to talk to us about the array. Or, at least, they want to talk to *you* about it. Now, as your agent, I've been stalling them as much as possible. But they're getting impatient. They want to know the location."

"I've told them the location," Pete said, scratching his arm distractedly. "It's on Earth."

"Earth's a big old planet. They want to know where exactly. You do know, don't you? You're not yanking my chain on this, are you? Maybe you should tell me what that soldier dude showed you in the cell."

Pete hesitated. There was something disconcerting about Xander's pushiness. Not for the first time, Pete wondered what would have happened if Private Ross had confided in Xander and not him. Would they still be here together? Or would Xander have simply abandoned him and saved his own skin?

"You're a smart kid," the YouTuber said, nodding as he saw Pete's reluctance. "Better not to trust anyone."

"Not even you?" Pete asked, surprised. He felt like Xander was doing the mental jiu-jitsu thing on him now.

"Especially not me!" Xander grinned. Pete had never noticed how pointed and sharp his teeth were, like they belonged to a wolf. He couldn't shake the feeling that, if there was ever nothing else to eat, he might find himself on the menu. He remembered how easily Xander had abandoned his teammates in Strike Force and shuddered.

"What you have is information, kid. And information is power."

"So, what happens next?"

"Well, the Red Eyes need us to throw them something. Some red meat, something that'll keep them happy. The trick is to give them just enough to satisfy them without giving them everything."

"Should I lie to them?"

"No, don't do that. It's too risky." Xander paused a moment. "Did that soldier tell you where the array is exactly?" His eyes flashed dangerously.

This, Pete thought to himself, is the first test.

"He gave me some information about where to find

it," Pete replied coyly. He bit the inside of his cheek, desperate not to blurt out the key piece of the puzzle. He'd never been any good at keeping secrets.

"Good," Xander said approvingly. "That's exactly the right answer."

The two boys stood in silence a moment. Xander spoke first.

"Do you know what's going to happen when we get to Earth? Scratch says the Red Eyes won't be able to stay hidden. They can't just sneak onto the planet and power up this array thing without anyone knowing. It's going to take time to get it all set up and operational. It could be months, maybe years. They'll have to reveal themselves."

"You mean they're going to invade the Earth?"

"'Invade' is a pretty strong word. It's more like 'temporarily occupy'. At least until they get what they want. They're gonna use the gamers from Hosin their shock troops. Can you imagine? No on want to open fire on a bunch of kids. The ged. lead the attack and then the Red Eyes wi' mop up the rest."

Pete gulped. He wasn't sure
But he hadn't expected th
of panic.

"They're going to need someone to help them negotiate terms on Earth," Xander continued. "A middleman." He smiled that smile again.

"You mean, you?"

"Like I told you, kid, I'm a dealmaker. I convinced them that they needed a human face to show people. If the emperor goes on TV and starts giving orders, everyone will freak out. They need someone with charisma. They want me to be their frontman."

Pete fell silent, deep in thought. If this was going to work, he needed to give out the information Private Ross had told him in dribs and drabs. But how could he string it out? He remembered what the soldier had said about UFOs visiting Earth and the crazy theory that the ancient wonders of the world were built with the help of aliens. He didn't have to tell the Red Eyes everything at once, he supposed. He could just give them a little bit at a time. Keep them busy. If he could buy Earth enough time before the array was found, the government or the military or someone would ~k out how to fight back against the invaders.

hu₁₁ you ever heard of the Chariots of the ‑ked Xander. The YouTuber shook his ‑s told me that the Squids helped ‑t wonders of the world. They were like caretakers, sent to help us evolve."

"Dude was nuts."

"He said the Squids helped humans build special sites all over the planet."

"What kind of special sites?"

"Things like the pyramids in Egypt and South America. Or the giant heads on Easter Island. The humans they met back then thought the Squids were gods and their spaceships were chariots that carried them up and down from heaven."

Xander moved closer to Pete, his eyes intense. "Tell me more."

"Well, he said they hid the array under the monuments. It's in sections, all over the planet, with one key control centre."

Xander pursed his lips. "It's going to take a long time to examine every one of those sites."

"I know. I'm sorry," Pete muttered.

Xander grinned, flashing those teeth again.

"Don't be sorry. Don't be sorry at all. It means we'll be useful for a while. If the Red Eyes are going all over the planet searching for the array, they'll need someone to smooth the way for them. This is the best answer you could have given me."

Pete waited for Xander to continue but the boy

seemed to be finished "Aren't you going to ask me for the list of locations?" he asked. "I thought you'd want to know."

Xander clapped him on the shoulder and smiled that unnerving smile.

"No, kid." He shrugged. "You're the key to that information. Keep it safe and give it out a little at a time. Like I said, information is power. But it's also dangerous. I've seen what the Red Eyes do to people. Mind control, torture devices…" He shook his head. "If I don't know where this thing is, they won't bother me."

"But they might torture me?"

Xander shrugged. "It's always possible."

Pete shivered. He suddenly felt more alone than ever.

26

IT'S A SHIP. BUT IT'S ALSO A BOMB... IT'S A BOMB SHIP!

Casey and the Reapers were silent as their shuttle headed out across space in pursuit of the Red Eyes' planet-killing bomb. After the dreadful decision they'd been forced to make, they were all lost in their own thoughts, their faces grim.

Across the empty void of space the Arcturian fleet assembled in formation in preparation for the jump to Earth. It looked like an intergalactic armada. Racing in the opposite direction towards Hosin, Casey felt a pang of uncertainty.

What if she was making the wrong decision?

Eldreth had said she was a caretaker, just like the Bactu. But who was she supposed to take care of?

Hosin? Earth? Her brother?

She couldn't do everything.

She looked down at the tranquil surface of Hosin, remembering Xolotl's kindness towards them and Eldreth's sacrifice in the arena. If the Squids had spent their lives helping other races, including humanity, that was a debt that needed to be repaid. And the Ghost Reapers were the ones, right here and right now, who had the opportunity to do that.

Although the boys weren't party to Casey's internal debate, they could see the conflicted emotions running across her face. They all felt the same sense of loss. Not just the death of Eldreth, Lieutenant Dreyfus and Private Ross, who'd all sacrificed their lives to save them, but also of Pete, who they'd somehow lost to Xander and the Red Eyes.

The whole team felt changed by what had happened since they first met in the shopping centre just a day or so ago. They had learned, Casey thought to herself, that real life came with consequences. There were no respawns. No checkpoints that let you go back and try a different path. Your decisions – good or bad – had permanent consequences.

As Casey changed out of her broken infiltrator suit back into her own clothes, Cheeze put the position of the bomb on the main screen so they could all see their progress as they chased after it. A secondary screen showed the Red Eye fleet around the space station and the team watched in astonishment as the ships started to vanish one by one. The light seemed to bend around the enormous vessels before they streaked forward and disappeared. The last one to vanish was the space station itself, heading to take up position in orbit around the Earth.

Without the hulking ships, the stars seemed to twinkle more brightly than before, as if a sinister presence had been removed.

"They must be jumping to light speed," Brain said.

"This is some next-level *Star Trek* biz," Elite mumbled. "Not gonna lie, every time I see something like that, I have to pinch myself to check this is real. We're on an alien spaceship, somewhere far across the galaxy, fighting to save a planet from getting blown up. My mind is melting here."

"But just think of the lyrics you can get out of it," Brain said, trying to lighten the mood.

"It's harder than you think. I'm, like, totally stuck right now. I can't even find a basic rhyme. I've got distance, existence, resistance. I need one more to make it all work."

"You'll get it eventually," Brain said, patting his shoulder. Talking about rapping was almost as bad as having to listen it as far as he was concerned.

It took them thirty minutes to catch up with the bomb. The planet-killer looked, to all intents and purposes, like an ordinary spaceship. Its body was long and thin with a semi-circular pod upfront that contained its flight navigation systems and a large cargo bay slung underneath that held the payload. It was designed to fly itself to its destination without a crew. Or, more precisely, it was designed to fly itself *into* its destination and explode on impact.

Casey had heard about the bomb ship in *SkyWake*'s lore, although it had never been spotted in the game. She knew that when it hit the target planet, it would release an explosion so intense it would tear the atmosphere apart. Even if the Squids survived the impact by staying hidden below the surface in their underground cities, the aftermath would kill them all as Hosin was turned into an airless rock.

The Reapers stared at the bomb ship on the main screen. It was hard to get any sense of its speed, but its size was clear. The planet-killer dwarfed their shuttle. As they approached, the ship's weapons turrets swivelled towards them, alert to their presence.

"Hate to say this," Cheeze announced, "but we won't be able to get any closer. That thing is spiky."

"I thought you said it was a bomb ship, not a gunship," Elite muttered, eyeing the automated guns uneasily as if they were pointed directly at him.

"It's designed to be antisocial," Cheeze explained. "If we get too close, it'll treat us as a threat. There's not even a docking bay. It doesn't like visitors."

"That's bad, isn't it?" Fish asked, although he already knew the answer.

"Can we hail the crew?" Casey suggested. "Try and convince them to stop?"

"There isn't a crew," Cheeze continued. "It's run by artificial intelligence, like a kamikaze automated pilot. The AI doesn't care if it lives or dies. It just wants to finish its mission and go *kaboom*."

Everyone took a moment, staring at the screen in silence as they wondered what to do next.

"I saw this movie once where these astronauts had to talk an intelligent bomb out of blowing itself up," Brain said.

"How did they do it?" Casey asked.

"They chatted to it about philosophy. Descartes and stuff. They tried to convince it that it didn't really exist."

"That's right smart that is," Fish said, tugging on the back of Cheeze's chair. "Get it on the comms, Cheeze. Tell it we want to talk about 'I think, therefore I am.'"

Casey bit her lip uncertainly. "Did it work in the movie?"

"Well, they convinced the bomb not to trust its sensors and made it question if what it could see was real or just a figment of its imagination," Brain explained. "But then the bomb decided that nothing existed other than itself. So, it ignored the astronauts, claimed it was God and said, 'Let there be light!' Then it blew itself up."

"Cancel the comms, Cheeze!" Fish yelled in a panic. "Don't tell it anything!"

"Can't you just hack into it, bruv?" Elite asked.

Cheeze spun his chair around. "Why does everyone always expect me to hack stuff? Oh, look, there's a locked door, Cheeze'll hack it. There's a drone, Cheeze'll hack it. There's a—"

"Blocked toilet," Fish suggested with a grin.

Cheeze shoved him.

"We need to get onboard," Casey said, trying to focus their attention back on the task at hand.

"How? I thought we couldn't dock?" Fish asked, confused.

"We've got spacesuits, haven't we? We could spacewalk across to it and get inside."

"No way," Fish replied. "No way am I wearing a spacesuit."

27

A STITCH IN TIME SAVES RHYME

There were only three Arcturian spacesuits on the shuttle, which meant Fish got his wish to stay behind. He wasn't alone. Since Cheeze's new hoverchair wasn't suited to the airless vacuum of space, he volunteered to stay behind too. He would monitor their progress and guide them at the console, just as he'd done when he'd hacked into the CCTV cameras in the shopping centre.

That seemed like a lifetime ago now, a distant dream, even. Casey's new reality was here in this universe of aliens and drones and strange powers that she didn't yet know how to control. She thought of her grieving mum back home, and she thought of Pete among the Red Eyes. Her whole family had now been torn apart not once, but twice.

As Casey, Elite and Brain pulled on their spacesuits,

Brain ran through the details one last time. The trip from the shuttle to the bomb ship would take the three astronauts across a vast expanse of space. Their suits, fitted with thrusters, would help them navigate the void.

The biggest challenge, which Casey realized as soon as the shuttle airlock opened, was a psychological one. She found the thought of taking that first step into the zero gravity of space terrifying. The star-studded blackness seemed to stretch for an eternity in all directions. The only sound was the rhythmic hiss of her suit's air supply as it kept her alive.

Her stomach flipped as she pushed herself out of the airlock.

Please, she prayed, *don't throw up inside your helmet.* She didn't fancy having to squint through a curtain of vomit for the rest of the mission.

Brain and Elite followed behind, silent with concentration.

From up here, the Squids' home world looked incredibly beautiful. Its azure seas glinted in the light from the two suns. Its land masses, their contours unfamiliar, were streaked with forests and mountains. There were no cities to be seen on the surface. In fact, the planet was completely pristine.

Casey wondered how many Squids lived down there. Millions, perhaps even billions. The idea of the bomb striking the planet, wiping out all its life as it stripped away the planet's habitable atmosphere, struck her more forcefully than it ever had before. No one had stopped the Red Eyes invading and destroying other planets, but she vowed she wouldn't let it happen here ... or on Earth. Someone had to stop them. Someone had to make a stand.

She clicked the thrusters on her suit, letting the jets fire for just a second or two to propel her forward. In space, Brain had told her, you kept on moving until you either hit something or changed direction. You didn't need to burn through the thrusters' fuel to move in the direction you were facing. Just a few bursts would be enough to propel you.

Over her shoulder, in the corner of her peripheral vision, she could see Brain and Elite. Their Arcturian spacesuits, like hers, were slightly too big for them.

"This is freaking me out," Elite complained into the comms. "Space is, like, so empty."

"I thought you didn't like *small* spaces," Brain countered. "This is wide open."

"That's the problem. It's *too* big." The boy stared at the vast emptiness through his visor.

"I'm with you," Casey agreed. "It's giving me the fear."

"I really like it," Brain said. "It's like scuba-diving or something. You know you're just a visitor out here. You can't stay for ever."

"You're weird, bruv. You know that?"

Landing on the bomb ship was trickier than they expected. Casey was the first to reach it, slamming into the ship's upper hull and grabbing hold of the base of a tall antenna tower to stop herself from spinning off. She fumbled with her spacesuit's wire tether as she clipped herself on to the tower, struggling to secure it with her chunky gloves. The tether clicked into place just in time for her to grab Brain as he spun past. He was travelling so fast that the movement pulled her off the hull, but the line caught her and pulled taut, and she managed to keep a grip on her friend's arm. They floated back into the ship's hull just in time to see Elite hurtling towards them.

"I'm coming in too fast," the boy yelled over the comms.

"Reverse your thrusters!" Brain warned.

It was too late, their teammate sailed right past them, out of control. He flew over the top of the ship and clipped the side of a huge satellite dish attached to the hull. Casey flinched, expecting to hear a thud, before realizing that there was no sound out here in the vacuum of space. Somehow the lack of noise made the impact seem even worse.

Elite spun out of control, getting further and further away from them, turning head over heels as if he was cartwheeling through the stars. Casey caught a glimpse of something red inside his helmet. Was that blood?

"Elite!" she shouted into the comms. No response. "Is he knocked out?" she asked in panic, wondering what damage the impact had done. She just prayed his suit had been able to withstand the blow.

"He's moving too fast," Brain told her. "Even if he's conscious, he won't be able to make it back. He won't have enough thrust."

"What can we do?" she asked. Every second they delayed, Elite was floating further away from them. "Cheeze, can you fly to him?"

"Not without triggering the bomb ship's defences, and if we try to go the long way around, he'll run out of oxygen before we get to him."

Casey eyed the gun turrets pointed towards the shuttle. The bomb ship knew the shuttle was there. If Cheeze piloted the shuttle any closer, it would open fire.

"What can we do, Brain? Think of something!"

Her friend didn't answer. He was focussed intently on Elite's trajectory, his lips moving like he was trying to work out some difficult puzzle.

Casey wished she could feel the same power she'd felt before. She wanted to be able to raise her hands and stop Elite, but her focus was gone, frayed by fear. While her mind raced, Brain untethered himself then bent his knees and launched himself up the antenna tower. He flew high above her, the momentum carrying him towards the top of the structure.

"Wait!" Casey shouted. "You're going the wrong way!"

She watched in confusion as Brain balanced himself on the side of the tower. Then he pushed himself off, firing his thrusters to propel him forward. It took her a moment to realize what he was doing. He had positioned himself so that his path would intersect with Elite's trajectory before he got too far away. It was a genius plan.

"Elite, can you hear me?" Brain called over the comms, his voice tense, as he floated towards the boy. There was no reply. Casey was struck by his concern. She'd always thought the two teammates drove one another crazy. She watched from the hull of the Red Eye ship as Brain closed in on Elite. He was still spinning somersaults. Brain's thrusters fired a second time, quickly on and then off, as he got himself into position.

He reached out to grab Elite, but the boy's speed made him hard to stop. Brain's gloved hand fumbled over his arm without getting a grip.

"No!" Casey cried, the word echoing hollowly inside her helmet.

She watched as Brain tweaked his thrusters, repositioning himself for a second attempt. The thrusters puffed gently, breathing out a burst of nitrogen that propelled Brain forward.

Puff! Puff! Puff!

Casey watched as Brain closed in on Elite. Closer. Closer. There!

Brain grabbed his friend's arm and, in a swift movement, hooked his tether on to Elite's suit. There was a jerk as the line between them pulled taut, but Brain fired his thrusters to compensate, fighting against Elite's forward momentum.

"He's got him!" Casey yelled over the comms. She heard Cheeze and Fish cheering inside the shuttle over her headset.

"He's not responding," Brain's voice cut in sternly, silencing them all.

Casey watched anxiously as Brain sailed through space back towards the bomb ship, dragging Elite's lifeless body behind him. As Brain attached himself once again to the hull, Casey could see the situation was not good. Elite was unconscious, the inside of his helmet spattered with blood from a gash on his forehead. Crimson beads floated from the surface of the cut, coating the inside of his visor. Casey was relieved to see that at least the glass had stayed sealed and airtight despite the deep crack that ran down it.

Brain carried Elite in his arms towards the bomb ship's outer airlock. Casey cranked the external override lever and they stepped inside. As the door closed behind them, Brain quickly lay Elite on the floor. There was a hiss as air flooded into the airlock, repressurizing it. As soon as the lights on the control terminal flashed green, Brain unlocked Elite's helmet and then his own. He pulled off his gloves and touched the boy's pale face.

"That looks bad," Casey murmured in despair, seeing the bruising gather around the wound. "He must have hit his head on the inside of his suit when he crashed into the dish."

"We need to help him," Brain told her. "What can we do?"

"I don't know..." Casey wished she had answers. "Cheeze, does the ship have a med bay?"

"It's designed to fly without a crew. No med bay, no canteen, nothing. It only has minimal life support systems for when the engineers are servicing it. Lights, air and artificial gravity. That's it."

Casey looked up to see Brain holding his chunky Arcturian med tool in his hand. If you held it over an injured soldier in *SkyWake*, it would patch them back up.

But this wasn't *SkyWake*. This was real.

"Should I use it?" Brain wondered aloud, hesitating. "I mean, it works in the game, right?"

"Yeah, but on Red Eyes," Casey reminded him.

Brain stared at the tool and then at Elite. Their teammate's breathing was shallow. "Not doing anything isn't really an option, though, is it?"

It was another choice that felt like taking a leap in the dark, Casey thought. Use the tool and risk hurting Elite more; or do nothing and risk him dying. It was an impossible decision. They were all impossible decisions.

She looked at the med tool and shook her head.

"I've never played as medic and I don't know anything about that tool," she said. "You're our team's healer. Whatever you decide to do, I'll back you up. It's your call."

Brain took a deep breath. "What I like about playing medic in the game is it's all about head not heart. I like the strategy element of it, figuring out who needed heals and how to keep them alive. You need good situational awareness and, by healing people up, you can change the course of a match. It was never really about actually caring for other people."

"But now it is…" Casey said.

Brain was quiet for a moment. "Elite's the total opposite of me," he said. "A motormouth show-off who hates books and school and learning. Plus, he can't rap to save his life. Against all odds, though, we're friends."

The colour was draining from Elite's face. Brain looked at the med tool in his hands one more time. He pushed his cracked glasses up his nose and exhaled. "If we do nothing, he's gonna die for sure."

He pointed the device at Elite's forehead. There was a bleep as the screen on the back of the tool lit up. Brain tapped it just like he'd done a million times before in the game. Then a beam of light shot out of the device and moved over Elite's forehead. Brain kept it steady, willing it on. To Casey's amazement, the bloody gash on Elite's forehead began to knit together again.

"What's happening?" Cheeze shouted over the comms from the shuttle. "Is he all right?"

"The tool must stimulate red blood cells to create collagen," Brain mused aloud. "Interesting."

Casey watched as the wound on Elite's head continued to repair itself, leaving a neat scar surrounded by a few flakes of dried blood. Days of healing seemed to have happened in the blink of an eye. Elite groaned. Then he sat bolt upright in shock and looked around the airlock.

"Welcome back," Casey said shakily.

Elite looked from her to Brain, then spotted the med tool in Brain's hand. He grimaced. "What did you do to me? I feel like someone took a sledgehammer to my head."

"Hey, I just flew halfway across space to save you. Used up all my jet fuel. A little thank you for my persistence wouldn't go amiss."

"Thank you," Elite said and gave Brain an awkward hug. "Wait," he said, breaking away. "What did you just say? *Persistence?*"

"Yeah, it means not giving up even when things are difficult. Persistence. It comes from the French *persister*, which means to linger or remain—"

"YES!" Elite shouted. "Persistence!"

"Did he hit his head harder than we thought?" Casey asked.

Elite shushed her, then he started to rap. *"Red Eyes come at me, better have persistence, 'cos I don't let no aliens mess with my existence. Get you in my sights, take the shot, no matter what the distance. One shot, one kill, that's how we roll, better expect resistance."* He stopped and looked at Brain, beaming. "Nailed it."

28

CUT THE RED WIRE!
NO, THE GREEN WIRE!
WAIT, HAVE YOU CONSIDERED
THE YELLOW ONE?

The inside of the bomb ship was sterile and silent. As Casey, Brain and Elite stepped through the airlock, the ship's internal lights switched on in sections, as if sensing their presence. It was creepy. Casey shivered.

"I've got the schematics for the ship," Cheeze said in their ears. "It's a pretty simple design. All the AI systems are in the forward module. The bomb itself is bolted into the ship's cargo bay."

"Does the AI know we're here?" Casey asked.

"Yeah, but I told it you're a Red Eye maintenance crew, come to check on it. It's turned on the life support systems for you. Head down this corridor, then I'll guide you to the bomb bay."

As they walked down the corridors, the lights came on in front of them and turned off behind them automatically. They looked over their shoulders uneasily. It felt as if they were being stalked by shadows.

"I've got a bad feeling about this," Fish said over the comms.

"Try being here," Elite muttered.

Ahead, a terminal was affixed to the wall, its screen flickering with Arcturian symbols. Casey didn't know the language well enough to understand what they meant. But, judging by the bright red colour and their insistent flashing, they were a warning.

"What's it mean?" Elite asked, looking over her shoulder.

"Nothing good, I reckon," Brain muttered.

An Arcturian voice began to growl over the ship's intercom systems, robotic and insistent. *"Rthyl ucht ack!"* it said over and over.

"That's an evacuation order," Cheeze told them over the comms. "Looks like it saw right through my cover story."

"The AI must know we're not authorized to be here," Casey replied. "We'd better hurry."

They began to run towards the next set of doors.

As they passed through them, they heard a sudden and protracted hiss that made Casey's spine tingle.

"Put your helmets back on," she ordered.

"Why?" Elite asked. "What's wrong?"

"Just do it. Quickly!"

The boys fumbled with their helmets, fitting them back onto the necks of their suits. Brain clicked Elite's helmet in place, locking it tight. Elite returned the favour then tapped on Brain's helmet with his fist to tell him he was good to go.

"Oxygen levels dropping all over the ship," Cheeze said over the comms as the boys helped Casey put her own helmet on. "The AI is flooding every deck with nitrogen."

"That's poisonous, right?" Casey asked, looking at Brain for confirmation.

"A few breaths of pure nitrogen will kill you."

"It's trying to repel boarders," Cheeze warned. "You'd better move. Take the next left."

They continued to run towards the main module, following Cheeze's directions. Casey had never been on a ship like this in *SkyWake* and she had no idea what the AI was capable of. It had already taken out the key life support system. What else would it do to stop them from defusing the bomb?

As if in answer to her question, the red emergency lights beside the next set of doors began to flash in warning.

"It's shutting us in!"

The three of them hurried towards the doors as they began to close. Before they were halfway there, the corridor lights went out. The only illumination now was the repetitive strobe of the emergency lights. The AI was making this as difficult as possible for them.

"How much further to the bomb bay?" Brain shouted over the comms.

"Two more doors!" Cheeze yelled. "Go, go, go!"

It was easier to say than do. The suits were clunky and heavy, meant for space exploration not an Olympic sprint. Fortunately, the doors were equally slow: at a metre thick, and designed to withstand a hull breach, they closed at a snail's pace.

The Reapers ran through the gap in the first door comfortably. The second was closer. Elite stumbled, almost falling over, before he reached it, but Brain grabbed him and, together, they slid through the doors just as they snapped shut.

"Last door up ahead," Cheeze informed them as they dashed down the final corridor, breathless from the exertion. "The bomb bay should be just the other side."

To Casey's surprise, the final door didn't try to close on them. It hung open, temptingly. It was almost as if it was inviting them to enter.

"Maybe the AI's given up," Elite suggested, slowing down.

"AI doesn't give up. It doesn't get tired; it's always strategic," Brain said sharply. "That's why it's better than humans."

"You're wrong," Elite said, stepping through. "Humans are always better. We've got *emotional* intelligence."

"I guess we'll soon see."

The cargo bay was an open space about the size of a five-a-side football pitch, with a high ceiling that towered above them. A set of huge cargo doors were on one side. In the centre of the bay, taking up most of the space, was a huge metal cage the size of a shipping container. It was bolted to the floor.

"That's the bomb," Casey whispered, overawed by the enormity of the thing. It dwarfed all of them.

Inside the cage lay a mass of cables tied together in huge loops like unruly spiderwebs, and in the middle of *these* lay an enormous metal cone like the warhead on a missile, covered in Arcturian warning signs. The cables ran from this to a computer terminal fitted at the far end of the metal cage.

There was a rumble behind them and the floor beneath their feet began to shake. All three of them turned, seeing the heavy entry doors start to close. They were being trapped inside with the bomb.

"We're running out of time, guys," Cheeze warned over the comms. "The ship's about five minutes out from entering Hosin's atmosphere. If you don't evac before then, you're gonna go down with it."

Brain rested a hand against the bomb's outer cage. "We have to be realistic about this. There's no way we can defuse this thing in five minutes. It's too heavy to move, too complex to disarm. I'm sorry to say this, but..."

"Maybe we can just work out which wire to cut?" Elite suggested hopefully. "That's what they do in the movies, right?" His eyes scanned the web of wires surrounding the warhead. "Red wire, green wire or yellow wire? Or just cut all of them?"

"This is a planet-killing bomb," Brain muttered scornfully. "You don't just snip a wire to disarm it!"

"Well, if you've got a better idea, stop chatting and spill it..."

While the boys argued, Casey crouched beside the bomb and examined it. It wasn't designed to be dropped by a plane or shot like a missile. It was less sleek and yet more sinister than that.

She wished her dad was here. He'd know what to do. He'd spent his entire military career disarming weapons like this. Well, not quite like this, but close enough: the bombs he'd defused in Iraq and Afghanistan were weapons designed to hurt innocent people, just like this device.

She reached into the cage and touched the payload, resting her hand against the warhead. The thing radiated evil. It had no other purpose except death and destruction. It was a malevolent, vile thing, and she wanted to get it as far away from her as possible. She wished she could throw it away.

Throw it away... The words made her stop in her tracks.

She looked over at the enormous cargo doors that were designed to allow the payload to be taken on and off the ship.

Could she unload it?

At that moment, something caught her attention above her head, reflected in the glass of her helmet. She recognized the shapes instantly.

"Drones!" she shouted, as a dozen of the flying bots swooped into the cargo bay. Brain and Elite split, trying to find some cover. Brain drew his energy sword from the belt of his suit and fired it up. Elite unstrapped the sniper rifle from his back.

"Fish in a barrel," he boasted, lining up the first drone through his sights. As he did, a burst of hot plasma fire sent him diving onto the floor. *What?* he cried, miffed. "They've got weapons?"

"They're the ship's internal defences," Cheeze explained over the comms. "Of course they've got weapons!"

"You're the drone king," Elite replied. "Can't you hack them?"

"They're controlled by the AI. It'd take me hours."

There was a flash of light as Brain brought one of the drones down with his sword, slicing it in half. Three more whizzed around him, opening fire. He ran for cover behind a stack of storage crates.

Casey could see they were outnumbered. She needed to move. "I'm opening the cargo bay doors," she said into the comms.

"But that'll depressurize the whole room!" Cheeze replied. "It'll suck you all out into space!"

"It's the only way to get rid of the bomb."

She ran to the control panel, glad to see it was one she'd seen before in *SkyWake*. Her glove tapped the familiar symbols. She struggled to get it right. The suit was designed for an Arcturian talon not a human hand.

"Lock on to something solid!" she ordered her friends as the warning lights above the huge loading doors flashed. She clipped her suit's safety tether onto the floor grille at her feet, hoping it would take the strain. There was a judder as the doors began to open and the air inside the ship was sucked out into space. The change in air pressure was immediate and it knocked the Reapers off their feet with all the force of a hurricane.

Elite and Brain, tethered to whatever was closest, ducked as cargo crates tumbled across the bay and were pulled into the inky blackness. The drones followed close behind, spinning out of control as the void drew them into its airless jaws.

The only thing that didn't move was the bomb. It was bolted onto the ship's hull by huge steel pins.

"Casey!" Brain shouted over the comms, his voice panicked. "That thing's heavier than a JCB digger. There's no way you can move it."

"I just need to give it a hand," Casey said.

She took a deep breath. The air in her suit, recycled on an endless loop, tasted stale. She thought about what Xolotl had told her. That humans had a latent power they could tap into … if only they knew how. Then she remembered Eldreth's final words.

You're a caretaker, Casey.

He was right.

She *was* a caretaker. That's what being a leader was all about. It was about looking after others.

She stared at the payload. It was huge and evil and destined to cause misery and pain. She knew it was her job to stop it. Just like her dad before her. He'd always said he joined the bomb disposal team because it meant he could help people, rather than hurt them.

"You're almost out of time," Cheeze warned over the comms. "If you don't get out now, you're going down with the ship. No one will survive the explosion."

Casey thought of Cheeze sitting on the bridge in the shuttle with Fish, watching all this through the live feed from their spacesuits' cameras. It must all seem chaotic and uncertain. But it didn't seem like that to her. For the first time since they'd left Earth, she felt sure she was doing the right thing.

She remembered what her dad had told her about the "Long Walk". It was what bomb disposal experts called it when they headed towards an explosive device. It had been his version of flow, that strange feeling when you tune everything out and just do what you've got to do without thinking, without worrying about the outcome.

"When you make that walk, everything falls away," he'd told her. "It's just you and the bomb. You forget about everything else. You're there to stop it exploding, to stop people from getting hurt. Nothing else matters."

Casey stared at the bomb again. She turned off her comms and her helmet filled with eerie silence. She saw Brain gesticulating at her from across the cargo bay, his arms flapping as he shouted something she couldn't hear. She closed her eyes. If she was going to do this, really do this, she needed to focus.

29

THROW IT AWAY

Casey realized with a sinking feeling that she wasn't quite sure what to do next. She knew the bomb was bolted to the floor of the cargo bay by enormous, industrial metal bolts. It had been locked in place specifically to prevent accidents just like the one she was trying to create. How, exactly, was she going to move it?

She thought of *SkyWake*. In the game, the Squids had a special ability called Telekinesis that let them move objects with nothing more than their minds. She closed her eyes and thought about the bolts, visualizing them in her mind. What was she supposed to do? Think about them loosening? Imagine them breaking free? She wasn't sure.

Her forehead creased as she tried to think with force and intent. She opened her eyes again, hoping to see the bomb had moved. But it was exactly where it had been before.

She couldn't help but look at her friends. Elite was on his belly clinging to a floor grille. The sniper rifle, slung around his neck, was being pulled towards the open bay doors.

Brain was in trouble. He had hooked himself onto a cargo crate that was tied behind black netting. As the air from the ship was sucked out into space, the crates were being pulled towards the open doors, straining against the net that held them in place. The material was beginning to fray and Brain, realizing what was happening, struggled with the hook on his safety harness, desperate to free himself before the netting gave way and he was pulled into space.

Casey closed her eyes again and concentrated on the bomb.

She had to do this.

She imagined the bomb.

She imagined the bolts.

She imagined the bolts loosening and the bomb lifting off the floor of the cargo bay.

She felt the ground shake beneath her and opened her eyes expectantly, but the bomb still hadn't moved.

Instead, the netting around the cargo crates had

finally ripped. The heavy crates flew across the cargo bay towards the open doors as the last of the air was sucked out into space. Elite pressed his body flat to the floor as a crate tumbled over his head and smashed into the wall before vanishing into the vacuum beyond. Brain, who'd just unclipped his harness in time, was knocked sideways by a second crate. He spun across the bay unable to get a grip on anything solid. Casey could see both boys yelling inside their helmets and, as she turned her radio back on, she was greeted by the sound of utter panic.

"Help me!" Brain hollered as he was tossed across the cargo bay towards the open doors. Elite grabbed his hand as he passed, his safety line pulling taut as it took the strain of them both.

"I've got you!"

"Don't let go!"

Elite tried his best to hold on, but the force was too much. His grip slipped and Brain began to fly away from him. Casey screamed, thinking he was lost. But Brain grabbed the sniper rifle slung across Elite's back and it jerked him to a stop. He floated in mid-air, his legs pulled towards the doors as if he was being vacuumed up.

The rifle's strap held, but only just.

"Two minutes to planet fall!" Cheeze's voice said over the comms. "Guys, you've got to get out of there. If you wait any longer, you'll be in Hosin's atmosphere, and you won't be able to spacewalk back to us."

"We're not leaving until it's done!" Elite yelled, his voice cracked and shrill as he struggled to hold on with Brain pulling the gun on his back. "Finish it, Casey!"

Casey turned back to the bomb.

She knew what she had to do now.

She had to choose.

Save herself and her team. Or try and save Hosin.

What would a caretaker do?

She closed her eyes and felt her mind empty. It wasn't about being strong, she realized. It was about being focussed. She felt the same strange sensation she'd felt before. It was the one she remembered from the gun turret of the Rhino on Hosin and in the corridor of the space station when she'd flattened the Red Eye squads.

This time, though, she felt in control of the power that was surging through her.

Everything seemed to fall away. It was the feeling she got when playing video games. The sense that the real world had been muted and it was just you and the game. All your doubt, all the nagging voices in the back of your head, just vanished.

In her mind's eye Casey saw each bolt that was holding the bomb down. She saw the shape of them. She saw the impressions on their surface where they had been riveted into place and the glint of the cargo bay's lights reflected in the steel. She concentrated hard and, as she did, she saw the first bolt slowly turning. She could feel the solidity of it, even though she wasn't touching it. She watched the bolt free itself from its setting and then fly across the cargo bay before being sucked out into space.

She focussed on the next bolt and then the next, loosening each one in turn with her mind. There was no rush. There was no sense of time at all. She didn't know if she'd been here for ten seconds or ten decades. It didn't matter. Her brain didn't need to think about it any more than it thought about her dinner going cold downstairs while she was in the middle of a deathmatch on-screen. She was totally absorbed in the task. This was what flow was. It was about channelling all your attention onto just one thing, concentrating the power of your mind like a laser beam.

"You're doing it!" Elite cried over the comms, his voice barely registering in her ears.

The bomb was now floating, free of its bolts, in the

middle of the cargo bay. It hung in the air weightlessly, entirely in Casey's control. She twisted her wrist, and the bomb made the same twist in the air.

"Sixty seconds to planet fall," Cheeze said on the comms. "You've got to get rid of it, Casey."

She cocked her head on one side, watching the bomb spin.

"Forty-five seconds," Cheeze said. "Hurry up!"

"Casey!" Brain yelled, straining. "I can't hold on much longer!"

Casey twisted the bomb again, her teammates' voices failing to get through to her. It was like spinning a 3D object in virtual reality. The feeling of power took her breath away. It was like she'd levelled up in a video game.

Without warning, the strap on Elite's sniper rifle snapped and Brain flew towards the cargo doors.

"No!" Elite cried, unable to catch his friend.

Casey watched Brain tumbling out into space. The action seemed disconnected from her, as if she was watching an event that had already happened, long ago.

"CASEY!" Cheeze shouted over the comms. "Get a grip!"

Something about his tone resonated in her brain,

shocking her back into the moment. She jolted like she'd just woken while sleepwalking and found herself standing on the edge of a cliff. She raised her right hand and Brain slammed to a stop in mid-air. With her other hand, Casey flicked her wrist and flung the bomb across the cargo bay towards the open doors. The huge device hurtled out into space and spun off, now free of her control. Elite and Brain stared at her, unable to believe what they were seeing.

Buffeted by the last of the air as it escaped from the bay, Casey pulled herself over to the controls and punched the touchscreen. The heavy bulkhead doors slid together, sealing the bay shut. Elite collapsed on the floor, panting with exhaustion. Brain, still suspended by Casey's strange powers, hung in mid-air.

"You can put me down now, Casey," he said.

She lowered her hand and her teammate landed gently on his feet. Before anyone could speak, Cheeze's voice cut in on the comms.

"You're entering the planet's atmosphere!"

The bomb ship began to shudder, gripped by Hosin's gravity. As it plunged towards the alien planet, Casey realized they had lost their chance to escape. She opened her mouth to scream but no sound came out.

30

VALKYRIE NEEDS FOOD BADLY

Casey's awareness of the video arcade arrived in pieces, as if her senses were coming online one by one. The first thing she noticed was the smell. It was a musty, tangy scent that reminded her of sweat, boiled cabbage and orange peel all rolled into one. Then her fingers felt the carpet she was lying on. It was threadbare and grubby, its swirly red patterns pockmarked with blackened pieces of decades-old chewing gum.

She sat up, tasting the staleness of the air on her tongue. A shrill aural collage of bleeps and bloops echoed in the darkness as the arcade machines tempted her with their attract modes, playing on a permanent loop. She walked along the rows of cabinets, recognizing retro eighties and nineties favourites that she'd discovered through her dad: *Shinobi*, *Mortal Kombat*, *Street Fighter II*, *OutRun* and *R-Type*.

At the end of the row, a man was hunched over a *Space Invaders* cabinet.

"Dad?"

She ran over to him and felt his strong arms around her as he swept her up into a bear hug.

"Casey!" he said, his deep voice echoing around the dark interior of the arcade. "My Casey!"

"Where am I?" she asked as he set her down again. "What happened to the shuttle? Where are my friends?" Her mind was buzzing with questions. "I was on the shuttle, and it was crashing and... Is this heaven? Am I dead?"

"No," her dad laughed, his eyes creasing with mirth. "You're very much alive. Although, if I had to imagine what heaven looks like, then a room stuffed full of video games would be a pretty good bet."

"But how are you here?"

"You're thinking of me," he said, "and so here I am."

"Is this the mindscape?" Casey asked. "I'm on Hosin?"

Her dad nodded.

"Then you're not real," she said, feeling a wave of bitterness crash over her.

"I'm as real as your memories of me are real," he

said gently and took her hand in his. She fought back tears, unwilling to let them fall.

"I am so proud of you, Casey," he said, staring into her face. "You and your friends did something amazing. You stopped the bomb. You saved Hosin."

"But I got everything wrong!" Casey cried. "I lost Pete, and the Red Eyes are about to invade Earth. They're going to find the array and…" Her voice trailed off. "I've failed."

"No, you did what you thought was right and you sacrificed yourself to do it. That's why I'm proud of you. You put others first."

Casey looked at her hands, remembering the power she'd felt as she lifted the payload and threw it into space.

"I don't know what to do next, Dad. The Squids have unlocked some power inside me, and I'm scared I don't know how to use it. I'm scared I'm going to let everyone down. My friends, my brother, the Squids … you."

Her dad kissed her forehead. "You know exactly what to do. You just have to trust yourself. Like I always say, you need to—"

"Go with the flow," she said, finishing his sentence for him. He grinned, pleased. "It's so good to see you," she said, feeling tears brimming in her eyes again. "I've missed you so much."

She stared at the flashing arcade machines beside her for a moment, distracted by their flickering screens as she wiped her eyes.

When she looked back, her dad was gone.

Casey wandered the rows of machines in a daze, unsure what she was supposed to do next. Then she heard a shout from the far end of the arcade. The Reapers were crowded around one of the cabinets, busy playing a game. They seemed to have appeared out of nowhere.

"Casey!" Cheeze said, hovering over to her in his new chair. "We wondered where you were. Look, we're playing this four-player *Gauntlet* machine. It's totally retro."

He led Casey to a wider-than-usual cabinet where the boys were crowded around a set of joysticks and buttons. On the screen she saw their characters – a warrior, a wizard, an elf and a Valkyrie – exploring a dungeon full of monsters.

"Your elf died," Brain said apologetically as Cheeze returned.

"Hey, Casey," Fish said, motioning to the unattended joystick. "Jump on and play. "You'll be better than Cheeze. He keeps getting swarmed by ghosts and dying horribly."

Casey looked at her teammates, uncertain how they were all so calm.

"Are you really here?" Casey asked. She wasn't sure if the boys were real or just figments of her imagination too. The Bactu's psychic world was so strange. It was like being awake and dreaming at the same time.

"Yep," Fish laughed. "Didn't Xolotl explain it all to you?"

Casey realized the Squid was standing behind her. The ancient alien was in front of a *Time Crisis* machine, holding a light gun in her tentacles.

I don't know why anyone would think this is fun, Xolotl said, blasting bad guys on the screen with impressive accuracy. *Sometimes I wonder if you humans are more similar to the Arcturians than we realized. You like fighting more than you like working together.*

"We're nothing like the Arcturians," Casey protested. "Surely we've proved that to you by now?"

Yes, I think you have, the Squid replied softly. She slithered away from the arcade machine, letting the game play on without her.

"How did we get here?" Casey asked. "The last thing I remember is the bomb ship hurtling towards Hosin."

The ship landed in the ocean. We rescued you from the wreckage.

"And the bomb?" Casey asked, trying to remember what had happened.

It's floating in space. It can't hurt anyone now, thanks to you.

Casey sighed with relief. "You were right," she murmured. "About me needing proper training. I'm sorry I didn't listen to you. I'm sorry about Eldreth, too."

Xolotl reached out a tentacle and touched Casey's cheek gently.

It's not your fault. We know you tried to protect Eldreth, just like you protected us. The Squid stared at Casey a moment, as if sensing a change in her. *How did it feel when you freed the bomb?* the alien asked.

"Powerful," Casey said, remembering the sensation she'd felt as she'd lifted the device into the air. She'd felt like a superhero. Capable of doing anything. But she also remembered the allure of the power, the feeling that her thirst for it might overwhelm her. The sensation had made her feel giddy and reckless, forgetting who she was for a moment.

Power can be intoxicating, addictive, the Squid said. *The Arcturians discovered that too. The more powerful they became, the more careless they were. They talk of honour and glory, but all they thirst after is power.*

"How do I control it?" Casey asked, shifting her weight from one foot to another. "I want to stop the Arcturians, not become like them."

It will take time.

"I don't have time!" Casey cried, angry at the Squid's soft-spoken lack of urgency. "The Arcturians took my brother! I didn't go after him so I could help you, and now he's heading to Earth with the Red Eyes. Who knows what they'll do to him when they get there?"

You want to go after them?

"I have to!" Casey declared. "For the sake of my family, my friends, my home."

Casey saw understanding and acceptance in the alien's ancient eyes.

You realize we don't have ships? We don't have a space fleet that can help you. It's been a thousand years since we last crossed the galaxy. Our time is over.

"We'll take the Red Eye shuttle," Casey said impatiently.

Xolotl regarded her a moment. *We will get it ready for you. In the meantime, you can rest here. Take a moment. For your friends' sakes, if not your own.*

Xolotl pointed a tentacle towards the boys crowded

around the *Gauntlet* machine. Casey realized that she was responsible for them, too. It felt like she was responsible for everyone.

"Casey!" Elite shouted, looking over his shoulder to see where she had got to. "We need your mad skillz! Get over here!"

Casey smiled to herself and headed back to join them. Xolotl slithered behind her, the alien's enormous body and tentacles out of place among the arcade cabinets.

Casey had never played *Gauntlet* before, but it was incredibly simple to grasp. The cabinet was wider than most arcade machines to accommodate joysticks and buttons for four players. Even so, you were forced to squeeze in around the screen shoulder to shoulder with your friends. She quite liked how that made you feel, all in it together.

Casey's avatar was an elf who could shoot arrows. Brain was a fireball-throwing wizard, Elite was a warrior, and Fish was a Valkyrie, the only female character. Cheeze hovered behind them, watching over their shoulders, beside Xolotl.

The game was a dungeon crawler. You were supposed to work together exploring a vast dungeon, looking for the exit to the next level while fighting hordes of ghosts, demons and weird little guys who threw boulders at you. The trick was to stay together and pick up food to keep your health up. But food was scarce and, if you weren't careful, you could accidentally shoot it before your teammates grabbed it.

The Reapers played in silence for a few minutes and the only sounds came from the game cabinet. It had a bunch of crackly, slightly sarcastic, speech samples that the AI dungeon master fired off now and then – *"Let's see you get out of here!"* or *"That was a heroic effort!"*

As their characters searched for treasure, Elite opened a door and accidentally released an enormous pack of angry ghosts that swarmed towards Fish's fighter. The Valkyrie's health meter rapidly dwindled as she took hits from all sides.

"Help me!" Fish shouted, waggling the joystick and hammering the buttons.

"Blue Valkyrie needs food badly," the AI dungeon master said.

They all cracked up at that, apart from Fish, who stared glumly at the screen as his Valkyrie died with a mournful groan.

"What's so funny?" he demanded.

"You died from lack of food. That's so on brand

for you, Fish," Cheeze said. "So on brand you could almost call it 'fishy'."

"You losers," Fish grunted. "I can't help it if I have a fast metabolism. I've been starving ever since we left Starbucks in the shopping centre." He glared at his team a moment then cracked a big grin. "Hey, I've just realized something. If we're going home, I can finally get something proper to eat."

While the Squids prepped the shuttle for its return to Earth, Casey and her friends stayed in the arcade. They knew it wasn't real, but, after all they had been through, they welcomed its familiarity. Xolotl even played a round of *Gauntlet* with them. Despite her age and what she'd said about video games, Casey got the sense she enjoyed it. She was particularly good at annoying Fish, shooting the food in the dungeon so that his Valkyrie couldn't regain her full HP.

Playing together like this, in co-op mode, Casey remembered what it was about video games that she loved so much. They weren't just about what happened on-screen. They were also about what happened off it. The fun of playing with friends and sharing a virtual world with them.

"I guess games for us are like the mindscape is for you," she told Xolotl as they finished up. "They give us a chance to share a made-up world together. Where we can be whoever we want to be and do things that we could never do in real life."

Xolotl nodded, her ancient face impossible to decipher.

"Well, I don't want to share any world with you guys," Fish harrumphed. "You're the worst to play with. Especially you," he added, jabbing an accusatory finger at the Squid.

Xolotl glanced around the arcade. *Maybe you'd prefer to play something else?*

"Like what?" Fish asked.

How about "Dance Dance Revolution"? the alien suggested, waving her tentacles towards a garish machine blasting out pop music.

Casey and the boys looked at one another in disbelief.

"For real?" Fish asked. "Squids can dance?"

Oh yes, Xolotl replied. *We Squids can bust a move.* Her tentacles undulated with amusement.

It took an hour for the Bactu to finish prepping and refuelling the Red Eye shuttle. As soon as it was ready, the Reapers left the mindscape and the Squids carried their sleeping bodies through the hot, humid tunnels that led from their underground nests. The shuttle had been placed on a wide plateau on a craggy stretch of mountains topped with snow. When the Ghost Reapers came to, they found themselves alone, lying on a patch of grass on the mountainside in the warmth of the two suns. The Squids had slithered shyly back underground leaving nothing but a few sticky trails on the ground.

Casey shook off the foggy head that always seem to accompany leaving the mindscape and looked out across the empty fields and distant forests. There was no sign of the beach they'd first landed on. All she could see was a beautiful and unblemished landscape without a single road or building to spoil the view. She guessed that the Squids, burrowed deep in their underground lairs and sharing their strange psychic dream-space, had no need to ravage the planet's surface with cities and spaceports.

She envied the closeness they shared. Everyone was constantly linked together, working for a common good. Still, she couldn't imagine staying underground all the time. The warmth of Hosin's two suns on her face, after all they'd been through in space, was invigorating.

"Casey," Cheeze said softly, hovering beside her. "We're good to go."

She took one last look at the strange landscape, then turned to the shuttle. "Do you even know how to get us back?"

"The Squids have programmed the course for us," Cheeze explained. "We're just passengers. It's a one-way ticket." He fell silent for a moment. "I'm sorry about Eldreth. Dreyfus and Private Ross, too."

"I know," Casey said. "They died so we could be here. They're heroes."

"We're going to get Pete back," he told her. "I promise you. We won't let Scratch and the Red Eyes win. Not after everything that's happened. They can't."

Casey hoped he was right.

Once everyone was strapped into their seats on the bridge of the shuttle, Cheeze pressed the launch sequence and the ship blasted off. It felt anticlimactic. There was no send-off party. No grand goodbyes. Just Hosin, on the big screen, slowly receding into the distance as the shuttle headed out into space. Casey wondered if she would ever see Xolotl again.

"Everybody ready?" Cheeze asked as the shuttle left the planet's atmosphere and the navigation system flashed in preparation for the jump to hyperspace. "It's gonna feel bumpier than the Red Eyes dropship. We're quite a bit smaller."

The boys sat back in their padded seats, ready for the inevitable jolt as they made the jump. Cheeze's hoverchair was locked in place, magnetically anchored to the floor of the bridge.

"On your mark, Captain," Cheeze said, looking at Casey. The rest of the boys followed his gaze, waiting for her to give the order.

"Do it," she instructed.

Cheeze hit the control panel and the ship shot forward. Casey felt the air around her tingle and tighten and the shuttle raced on, the stars on the viewing screen stretching into long, unbroken lines of white light. She gripped the armrests on her seat as she was forced backwards.

They were finally heading home.

31

YOU HAVE REACHED
YOUR DESTINATION

Darkness. That was the first thing Casey saw. A vast, impenetrable darkness that was so black it made her panic. She brought one hand up to her face to convince herself that she was still there. She was. But she had no idea where "there" was. Or even which way was up, and which way was down. The darkness was total. She imagined this was what it was like to be blind.

"Who's that?" Brain's voice said. He was so close that she felt his breath on her neck. She turned, reaching out a hand.

"Brain?"

"Casey?"

Their fingers brushed in the gloom.

"Hey! Who turned out the lights?" demanded a familiar Scottish voice.

"Hold on, everyone," Cheeze said somewhere near by. A torch on the side of his hoverchair switched on, its narrow beam cutting through the darkness and lighting up a corner of the shuttle's bridge. From what Casey could see, the ship was a wreck. All of the terminals were offline, and several were emitting fine trails of smoke that had the tainted, metallic smell of burned electrics.

"Something must have happened in the jump," Cheeze said, looking at the chaos.

"Did we hit something?" Elite piped up.

"I think the damage is from the impact," Cheeze said.

"What impact?" Casey asked. She wasn't aware they'd hit anything.

"Our landing," Cheeze told her, pointing to the shuttle's windscreen. "Look…"

Although it was dark outside, they could see that they were no longer in space. They were on the ground in what looked like a park. Green grass, well manicured, stretched out in front of them towards a thick English oak tree.

"We're home!" Casey shouted, unzipping herself from her seat.

"The nav computer must have misfired or

something," Cheeze said, inspecting the busted terminals. "Maybe I made a mistake setting it."

"It doesn't matter," Fish told him. "We're back. Home, sweet home. I'm gonna kiss the ground the minute we get out of here."

It took them a little while to work out how to open the shuttle's hatch, since it had lost power in the crash. While Brain, Fish and Elite forced the doors apart, Cheeze downloaded the nav system's data to his hoverchair and tried to work out what had happened during the trip. His face remained puzzled.

"It's not your fault," Casey told him as he pored over the data on the monitor attached to the arm of his hoverchair. He peered at the numbers, his lips moving silently as he absorbed the information.

"You're right," he said finally, looking up. "We hit a meteor storm as we made the jump to faster-than-light speed. Statistically, there's a billion-to-one chance of something like that happening. The nav systems are specifically designed to avoid them, but Xolotl did say the shuttle was smaller than the type of ship you'd usually use for this kind of journey."

"Judging by our luck so far, I'd say it was to be expected," Casey said, patting him on the shoulder. "Alien abduction. Check. Caught between two sides in an intergalactic war. Check. Hit by meteors. Check."

Cheeze frowned as he looked through the data on his screen. Then Brain came over and peered at it. His face fell.

"What's going on?" Casey demanded, sensing something bad was brewing.

"Do you want to tell them, or should I?" Cheeze asked Brain.

"I think you should. It's your data."

Cheeze sighed and spun his chair around to face everyone. He cleared his throat nervously. "It looks like our trip home took a little longer than expected."

"We know," Casey said. "We hit a meteor storm. We're just grateful you got us back in one piece. No one minds if we went the long way round."

Cheeze looked at Brain for help.

"When Cheeze says 'a little longer'," Brain explained, "what he actually means is *quite a lot longer*."

"Like how long?"

"Four years longer," Cheeze said.

"Wait, *what*?" Fish demanded. "You're saying we've been stuck in hyperspace for four whole years? But it only felt like seconds. You hit the button and we flashed forward and now we're here."

"I guess the drive system must create some kind of

Einstein–Rosen bridge, like a wormhole," Brain said, furrowing his brow. "It bends time and space to let you jump from one side of the galaxy to another in the blink of an eye." Fish and Elite exchanged a look, both unable to understand a word he was saying.

"We hit the meteor storm just as we made the jump and it threw the nav system off. The computer kept on jumping and jumping, trying to get us back to our original course by bending time and space. What felt like a minute to us on the deck of the ship actually took four years. By the time we made it to Earth, the ship was on its last legs, which must be why we crashed, I guess."

"That means I missed my birthday. Four times!" Fish said to no one in particular. "I've never missed my own birthday."

When the Reapers climbed out of the shuttle, they realized that they had landed in Hyde Park in Central London, late at night. The minute Fish stepped onto the grass, he instantly dropped to his knees and kissed the ground.

"Earth," he said, "I'll never leave you again."

The shuttle's arrival had been messy. The Arcturian ship had ripped across the lawns, leaving a trail of destruction behind. A few trees were smoking, charred by the heat from its engines as it landed. The shuttle had stopped with its nose resting against a marble fountain with a statue of a boy and a dolphin on top of it. The statue was leaning slightly, knocked off balance by the impact.

It took the Reapers a good half an hour to cross the deserted, pitch-black Royal Park. When they reached the ornate railings that lined its edge, they clambered over them one by one and found themselves on the streets of London's West End.

Blinking in the gloom, the teammates saw that Oxford Street was completely different from how they remembered it. The world-famous shopping street was now a bomb site. Every other building seemed to have been reduced to rubble. The road itself was ripped to pieces, lumps of tarmac thrown here and there and lying in precarious piles. It reminded Casey of the photos of London during the Blitz from her history textbook, the buildings smashed apart or flattened by the falling bombs.

Bricks and broken glass littered the pavements, and no one seemed to have made any effort to clear it up. Everything was eerily quiet. There was no traffic, nor any pedestrians. At Oxford Circus they saw a solitary man in a trench coat walking on the other side of the road. He kept his head down, his eyes locked on the mobile phone in his hand. Not even Cheeze's hoverchair got his attention.

"What's going on?" Casey asked. She felt a sinking feeling in her stomach. Dread and despair rolled into one. This wasn't the homecoming she had imagined. She wished they still had weapons, but they'd lost all their gear when the bomb ship had crashed on Hosin. She missed her plasma rifle.

"Look!" Fish cried, pointing to a familiar logo on the side of a fast-food chain restaurant. It was like a beacon in the darkness, wedged between wrecked buildings.

"We really don't have time," Brain muttered.

"Come on!" Fish complained. "Do you know how hungry I am? All that time in space, the only decent meal we got was an imaginary one. Let's go inside and we can ask them what's happening. I'm buying." He flashed his wallet at his teammates encouragingly.

The Reapers followed Fish as he ran across the rubble-strewn street and pushed open the door to the fast-food restaurant. The familiar interior should have been comforting, but there was something not quite right about it. There were no customers, and when Fish approached the counter he saw there were also no staff. The whole place was automated.

"*Please select your order on the touchscreen,*" said a voice on a computer terminal.

"Whoa," Elite said. "Since when did robots start cooking burgers?"

"There aren't any burgers," Fish said, looking at the menu in disgust. "All they're serving is nutritional paste, just like that muck we had in the space station. There's ten different flavours of the stuff according to this. I bet they all taste of cardboard."

"We should go," Casey said, anxiously. "Something's wrong here."

The Reapers turned to leave. As they did, a man and a woman entered the restaurant, dressed in black army fatigues and red caps. The woman had a plasma rifle strapped across her chest. The man carried a vicious-looking stun baton. They stopped dead as they saw the Reapers.

"What are you kids doing here?" the woman demanded, eyeballing them. "Only authorized citizens are permitted outside after curfew."

"Sorry," Casey said quickly. "We made a mistake."

"Show me your ID cards," the man said, his gloved hand tightening around the baton. The woman looked at Cheeze's hoverchair. Her lips pursed sourly.

"We didn't realize how late it was," Casey said,

thinking on her feet. "We'll head straight home now."

"Halt!" the woman ordered. "Prepare to be scanned." She held up a device and a lattice of lasers burst out and fell on Fish's face.

"Ow, that tickles!"

There was a beep as the lasers finished scanning his face. Not a satisfied beep, but the kind of annoyed beep that a supermarket checkout scanner makes when it rejects an item. Fish looked around nervously. "Did I pass?" he asked hopefully.

"We have a level-three infraction," the woman said into a radio mic on her tactical vest. She raised her plasma rifle and pointed it at the Reapers.

"You definitely failed," Elite told Fish.

The woman glared at them. "All of you, move over to the side and—"

"Run!" Cheeze yelled, shoving his hoverchair forward and barging straight between the two soldiers. He twisted sideways and burst through the doors onto the street. His teammates ran after him.

"Stop!" the soldiers shouted, but no one listened.

Oxford Street was still deserted. No cars. No people. Not even any buses or taxis. The Reapers realized they were on their own.

"This way!" Casey called, charging down an

alleyway. Her team followed, twisting and turning through the streets, running blind, until they emerged from a side street into the vast urban expanse of Piccadilly Circus. The iconic neon billboards hung high above the buildings, still functioning despite the damage to the rest of the intersection.

The Reapers drew up sharply as a newsflash filled the giant screen. It showed Red Eye troops and overseers on the ground at an archaeological site. Mechanical diggers and enormous cranes were excavating a pit around a familiar-looking structure in the desert while hundreds of human workers, fitted with shock shackles, toiled in the heat.

"That's the Great Pyramid in Egypt," Brain said, immediately recognizing it. Before he had a chance to say more, the footage cut to a grand briefing room with panelled wooden walls. A lectern stood on a podium facing the camera, and behind that stood a figure they couldn't mistake, despite the fact that he was four years older than when they'd last seen him.

"Xander!"

The YouTuber stared straight into the camera. He'd let his hair grow long and had a small goatee on his chin. He was flanked by two Red Eyes in power armour carrying plasma rifles.

"My fellow citizens," he said, smiling broadly, "today our Arcturian allies completed a successful excavation of the new dig site and discovered the fifth part of the psionic array. Our chief technical officer has carried out a full analysis of the new piece and is confident that he will be able to pinpoint the sixth and final location in due course."

The camera panned slightly to reveal Pete standing beside Xander. Casey stared in stunned silence as her brother's face filled the eight hundred square metre video screen overlooking Piccadilly Circus. He looked taller and more mature, no longer her baby brother. She blinked, not quite able to get her head around the fact that he was now the same age as her.

"With your help," Xander went on, "we will continue to aid our allies in their quest. For the glory of Arcturia." He held his closed fist to his chest in imitation of the Arcturian salute and smiled that charming, yet insincere smile that Casey had come to hate.

"What the hell is going on?" Fish demanded.

"We're late," said Brain. "This is what's happened while we've been stuck in hyperspace."

"That egotistical tool has finally got what he wanted: he's world famous," Cheeze said eyeing

Xander. "Shame he had to sell the whole planet down the river to reach his goals."

There was a rumble behind them. A Rhino rolled up, coming to a stop in the middle of the junction. The alien troop transport looked entirely out of place on this London street, especially with the statue of Eros silhouetted behind it. Four Red Eyes and two human soldiers wearing red caps climbed out, plasma rifles raised and ready to fire.

"Stop, or we'll shoot!" one of the human soldiers warned. The Reapers froze. More Rhinos were now pulling up, trapping the team in the middle of the intersection, beneath the electronic billboards.

Casey looked around wildly for a way out. Behind them she saw a stairwell that led down into Piccadilly Underground. The entrance was blocked by a padlocked metal gate covered in rust. It didn't look like it had been opened in years.

Before she could move, a ground-shaking series of thuds, like giant footsteps, could be heard across the intersection. A gigantic machine appeared, towering above the ruined buildings around Piccadilly Circus. It was at least fifteen metres tall and walked on long, thin legs that let it step over the bomb-blasted buildings with ease. Its body, framed against the night sky, was smooth and round like the carapace of a beetle.

The machine stopped and turned towards the Reapers, a searchlight shining from its undercarriage that lit them up like they were on the main stage at Glastonbury.

"What is that thing?" asked Cheeze in awed wonder, craning his neck to look up at it.

"Whatever it is, it's got us trapped!" Elite yelled, shielding his eyes from the glare.

"This way!" Casey ordered, taking control. She ran towards the stairwell that led into the Tube station. "We need to get underground."

"But the gates are locked!" Fish warned.

"I've got it," Casey said, stretching her hands out in front of her, her brow creased in concentration. There was a crunch as the gates were wrenched off their hinges and floated upwards, remaining suspended above the Tube entrance. The boys stared in amazement.

"Open fire!" a red-capped soldier shouted, and the assembled troops began to shoot. In one deft motion, Casey lifted her hands, spun the gates in mid-air and then threw them at the soldiers. The troops screamed as they were flattened beneath the heavy ironwork.

There was a crunch and a yawning sound of metal and hydraulics as the enormous machine came after them. It moved with a jerky yet speedy step, towering over the street. Casey saw a plasma cannon on its undercarriage power up, ready to fire.

"Move!" Brain shouted.

The team half ran, half fell down the stairwell into the Tube and reached the green-tiled tunnel that led into the ticket hall just as the cannon fired a searing blast of plasma. There was an explosive thud and the stairwell collapsed behind them in a cloud of masonry dust.

The Reapers stood inside the shadowy ticket hall and caught their breath. The boys all stared at Casey, still unable to quite believe what their friend was capable of. She could tell that her power disconcerted them as much as it impressed them. It disconcerted her, too.

"Where do we go now?" Cheeze asked. The place didn't look as if it had been used in a while. A thick layer of dust lay over the ticket barriers and there was no power for the lights. The chances of hopping on a train seemed slim.

"We need to get somewhere safe," Brain said. "If the trains aren't running, maybe we can head along the tunnels and avoid the patrols."

"But where is safe?" Fish asked, checking over his

shoulder nervously. "If the Red eyes have taken over the whole planet, we're stuffed."

"We'll figure something out," Casey said. She looked [at t]he boys, hoping they w[e]re with her. "Won't we?"

"...ly Ghost Papers always sort[ ]t out," Elite said, with a co[...] "Actually, I've got [a] rhyme about—"

"Save it for later," [...]n cut in.

"You're right, brai[...] It's gonna sound so much better echoing along the [...] tunnels. The acoustics will be sweet."

"Please, no..."

"We should move," Casey said, her voice calm and authoritative. "It won't take them long to get through that barricade." She jumped over the deactivated ticket barriers, heading into the dark belly of the underground station. She didn't need to look over her shoulder to know that her team would be right behind her.

TO BE CONTINUED

Acknowledgements

I'd *like to* say a huge thank you to the following people.
All of the amazing team at Walker Books in the
UK and Australia/New Zealand. I'm so honoured to
be published by you. My wonderful – and eternally
patient – editor, Emma Lidbury; designer Anna
Robinette; copyeditor Clare Baalham; Kirsten Cozens
and John Moore in Publicity and Marketing, and
everyone else who has worked on this book. James
Fraser, for his out-of-this-world cover art. My eyes
melted with excitement when I first saw it! My agent,
Ella Kahn, whose advice and kindness I'm indebted
to. Thank you all.

Everyone who supported *SkyWake Invasion.*
I've been incredibly touched by the generosity of
booksellers, bloggers, teachers, librarians and readers
in championing the first book in the series. Special

thanks to Kirsty Applebaum, Jo Cummins, Rachel Delahaye, Scott Evans, Kate Foster, Liz Hyder, Andrew Mills, Rashmi Sirdeshpande, Dan Smith, Karen Wall, all my fellow debuts in The Good Ship (what a talented and lovely bunch you lot are), The Rocketship Bookshop, A New Chapter Books, Cracked and Spineless Books (hello, Leo!), Pengwern Books, Waterstones Shrewsbury (and lots of other branches), Shropshire Bookfest and the super folk at Nerdy Coffee Co.

I'm also hugely grateful to BookTrust for including *SkyWake Invasion* in their School Library Pack for 2021/2022. It's been incredible to see my little story heading out to school libraries up and down the country.

Thanks to all my family and friends for their support – especially Mum, and Dad and Lorna. Thanks also to John and Anna Groombridge and to everyone I know who picked up a copy of *SkyWake* for their children or grandchildren (or sometimes just for themselves). You are the best.

Finally, huge thanks to Louise, Isobel and Alice. You guys are my dream team. I love you all more than you'll ever know.

Jamie Russell is a former contributing editor of *Total Film* magazine turned screenwriter and author. He has written several non-fiction books, including *Book of the Dead: The Complete History of Zombie Cinema* and *Generation Xbox: How Videogames Invaded Hollywood*. *SkyWake Battlefield* is the second in a trilogy, sequel to *SkyWake Invasion*.